MW00881217

Finding Miranda

IRIS CHACON

Happy reading.
Iris Chacon

Delia Stewart, Publisher
Miami, Florida USA

Library of Congress Control Number: 2016913162
Copyright © 2016 Delia L. Stewart
All rights reserved.
ISBN-13: 978-1-519400-24-6

DEDICATION

This book is dedicated to Bill Coppage, who will never
see this but who taught me more about life, radio, and
spirituality than almost anyone I know. He has been an
inspiration not only to this writer but to countless others,
both blind and sighted.
Thank you, Bill, and God bless you always.

CONTENTS

1 THE RITUAL

Seventy-five-year-old Martha Cleary relaxed in her front porch rocker by dawn's misty glow with her coffee at her side, her binoculars hanging from her neck, and her small-caliber rifle in her lap.

Wide, shady verandas were the norm in the tiny community of Minokee. The rustic frame houses crouching beneath the live oak trees were nearly as old as the trees themselves. No one had air conditioning in Minokee. With their Old Florida architectural design—all wide-opening windows and deep, dark porches—the quirky ancient cottages were cool even when it was hot enough to literally fry okra on the sidewalk downtown. If Minokee'd had a sidewalk. Or a downtown.

Next door—and only a few yards away from Martha Cleary's rocking chair—a screen door creaked open and whapped shut. Bernice Funderberg doddered toward her own rocker, blue hair in curlers, pink fuzzy slippers complementing her floral housedress.

"Yer late," Martha said.

"Yeah, when ya hit seventy ever'thing ya gotta do in the bathroom takes a durn sight longer than it yoosta," groused Bernice. "Did I miss 'em?"

"Nah, not yit." Martha lifted her binoculars and peered off down the narrow asphalt road to where it curved into the thick palmetto scrub a half-mile away. A jungle of vines,

1

palmettos, young pines, and broad, moss-draped oaks pressed close alongside the road. Nothing was visible through the tangle of flora and shadow. "They ain't made the turn yit. Prolly got a late start—like you."

"But not fer the same reason, I'll betcha!" Bernice said with a chuckle.

"Bernice, poop jokes is the lowest form of humor. I am appalled at your unladylike references to bodily functions at this hour of the mor— Get outta there, you sorry varmint!" Martha raised, cocked, and fired her rifle in one smooth, practiced motion. Bushes rustled in the garden bordering her porch.

"Git 'im?" said Bernice, unruffled by the sudden violence. It was just another dawning in semi-quiet little Minokee.

"I didn't wanna hurt 'im, jest wanted 'im outta my summer squashes." Martha set her rifle aside and shook a fist at the bushes. "Find yerself another meal ticket, Bugsy! I don't do all this yard work fer my health, y'know!"

Bernice snorted. "Yes, ya do, ya old biddy. Say, ain't that them?" She pointed toward the far curve of the road.

Martha hoisted her binocs, focused, smiled, and nodded. "Yep. Here they come."

"Shucks," whined Bernice. "Looks like a shirt day."

"Hush up, ya shameless cougar!" said Martha.

Across the narrow street, first one and then another screen door whined as other house-coated, coffee-carrying ladies emerged and took their seats in porch chairs. The new arrivals waved, and Bernice and Martha waved back, smiling.

"Jest in time," Martha said.

In the distance a man and dog loped toward the cottages, gliding along the leaf-shadowed, warm asphalt, with a soft whhp-whhp-whhp as the man's running shoes met the pavement. He wore faded jogging shorts that showed off well-muscled thighs. A tee shirt stretched across his wide chest and tightly hugged his impressive biceps. His pale beard was trimmed close to his face, which was shaded by the bill of his Marlins baseball cap. He wore sunglasses. His donkey-sized dog wore a bandana.

The ladies in the porch chairs sighed and sipped their coffee, all eyes devouring the oncoming duo. As he drew nearer, without slowing his pace, the man angled his face with its hidden eyes right and left and acknowledged each lady with a wave. A mellifluous bass voice rumbled from behind his pectorals, "Mornin' Miz Martha, Miz Wyneen, Miz Bernice, Miz Charlotte."

"Mornin' Shep, mornin' Dave," each lady called in turn. They did not wave back.

The running shoes whhp-whhp-whhpped past the ladies and on down the tree-arched road. The porch ladies rose from their chairs and turned to watch the eye-candy-in-a-ball cap move away from them. When Shep and Dave rounded the next corner, out of sight, all four ladies gathered their coffee cups, binoculars, and (in at least one case) weapons. With contented sighs, Martha, Wyneen, Bernice, and Charlotte went back into their respective homes. Even with a shirt, today had been a good day.

2 THE VISIT

Shepard Krausse's cottage was as ancient as the other Old Florida bungalows in Minokee, but unlike his elderly neighbors, Shep had not been living there since the Eisenhower administration. Shepard's flowerbeds were well tended and blooming wildly because he paid good money to minions he never saw. He grew no vegetables as Martha Cleary did, and even if he had grown them, he would have happily shared them with the local brown rabbits, no rifle required. He didn't have any particular political agenda regarding firearms; they just weren't for him.

Shep's running companion, Dave, did have strong opinions about the NRA and gun control, but nobody cared. Dave was a dog, for Pete's sake.

Shep banged through the back door, into his home's cozy kitchen. He wriggled out of his sweat-soaked tee shirt and dumped it into the washing machine just inside the door. Dave followed him in, sat down next to the washer, and looked up expectantly. Shep removed Dave's bandanna and added it to the dirty laundry.

Shep removed two water bottles from the fridge and poured the contents of one into Dave's dish. Uncapping the second bottle, Shep raised it in Dave's direction: "Cheers, Dave." Dave lapped at his bowl while Shep guzzled his bottle dry. Then Shep refilled both bottles at the sink and returned them to the fridge.

"Ready for a shower?" he said to Dave.

"Whff," replied Dave, using his indoor voice.

"Well, let's go, then," said Shepard and turned to precede Dave down the hallway to the bedroom and bath. Shep removed his Marlins cap, and a white-blond ponytail slid from beneath it, rippling down the center of his back. He did not take off his sunglasses.

As they passed the living room, Dave whirled to face the sofa. His ears snapped back against his skull, black lips curled, fangs protruded, and a deep, threatening rumble vibrated from his throat. Shep was beside the dog instantly.

"Who are you?" Shepard asked.

"Don't be alarmed, Mr. Krausse. And call off your dog, please," a calm, gravelly voice came from the stranger slouched into the deep sofa cushions.

Shep placed one hand on Dave's back. Dave stopped growling but neither retreated nor hid his fangs. "I'm not alarmed," Shep said, "but I am curious. What are you doing in my house? Did my mother send you?"

"Cute little town, Minokee," said the man casually. "People really don't lock their doors. You might want to rethink that. And, no, I haven't had the pleasure of doing business with the lovely and impressive Mrs. Montgomery-Krausse. I'm here on behalf of a, uh, concerned citizen. I have a message for you."

The huge dog might have been cast from bronze; he was still as death and just as scary.

Shep spoke lazily, but his body had shaken off the fatigue of his morning run in favor of all muscles tensed in high alert. "I don't believe I've done anything to, uh, 'concern' the citizenry. And I have a machine that takes messages. My number's in the book, Mr. ...."

The man hauled himself from the depths of the couch and stood. Coins jingled as the man's fingers fidgeted in his pocket. In the heat and humidity, the man's suit jacket smelled like a wet llama. Shep thought the air conditioner in the man's car must be broken.

"I didn't phone, Mr. Krausse, because you might not have listened to your messages. My client wants to be certain you hear and understand his concerns."

"Then tell me what they are, and get out."

The man presented his message in two crisp sentences, then said his farewells and backed out the front door, watching Dave all the while. Shepard kept silent, his restraining palm resting in the raised fur on Dave's back. The whole encounter had lasted less than ninety seconds.

Shep and Dave stood motionless until they heard a car crank to life and move off down the street. Shep then moved to the front door and locked the deadbolt. Only then did he respond to the stranger's two sentences.

"Like hell I will," was his whispered vow to the departed man—and to himself.

3 THE D.M.V.

An hour away from tiny Minokee, the bigger town of Live Oak steamed like broccoli in a microwave: green, limp, wet, hot, and fragrant. Summer was an infant according to the calendar, but the time-and-temperature sign outside the bank said baby had grown up fast. At barely nine in the morning it was already over ninety degrees in the shade.

Of course, no shade existed (and, for the moment, no air conditioning either) inside the cramped local office of the Division of Motor Vehicles. Miranda Ogilvy might have endured the heat better than most, with her skinny physique and sleeveless cotton sundress, but she was sandwiched between a buxom big-haired Hot Mama and a barrel-bellied, sweat-stained Good Ol' Boy. After languishing in the stagnant line of bodies for nearly an hour, Miranda's toes had been crushed by the platform heels of Hot Mama four times. Her heels had been bruised by the sharp-toed cowboy boots of G.O.B. three times. Neither neighbor seemed aware of Miranda, though she was pillowed between them like a slipped disc in a miserable spinal column.

Silently Miranda forgave her heavy-footed line-mates; it wasn't their fault. Nobody ever noticed Miranda.

"Next!" bleated an agent whose red face glistened between lank bangs and wrinkled shirt collar. Hot Mama peeled her backside off the front of Miranda's sundress, lifted her platform heels off Miranda's numb toes, and shuffled to the counter.

Oblivious to Miranda's presence, the crowd of humanity behind her surged forward, led by G.O.B.'s pointy shit-kickers. Miranda advanced two quick steps to avoid being trampled. Now at the front of the line, she luxuriated in breathing deeply since no one was plastered against her front from toes to sternum.

Two yards down the counter to the right, the previous customer departed, and Miranda leapt like a gazelle into the vacant spot.

"Next!" an empty-eyed public servant bellowed directly into Miranda's face. The woman was shorter and wider than Miranda and actually leaned to look around Miranda for the next victim.

"I'm here," Miranda said with a smile and a timid wave.

The official started and then focused on the front of Miranda's sundress. "How can I help you?"

Miranda pushed an envelope and her driver's license across the counter. "I need to change the address on my license, please."

"You can do that by mail or on-line, y'know." The tone of voice said, *It's lunkheads like you who cause long lines on hellish days like this!*

"I tried," said Miranda sweetly. "They said I need a new picture taken." She eased her driver's license an inch closer to the official, who looked down at it and frowned.

"Where's your face?"

"Right there in that rectangle, see?"

"That's not your face, it's the back of your head! You can't have the back of your head on your driver's license!" She angled her shoulders as if to talk over her shoulder, though she continued shouting directly into Miranda's nose. "Freddie, they can't have the back of their head on their driver's license picture, right?"

The shoulders squared up toward Miranda once more. "You gotta have your face in the picture, honey." Her eyes said, *What are you trying to pull, sister?*

"I know. They tried and tried. That's the best we could get. I'm sorry. I just don't photograph well," said Miranda. *I'm a sincere, law-abiding citizen, really, truly I am, and it's not my fault your air conditioner is broken and it's two hundred degrees in here.*

The squatty official pursed her lips, glared at the driver's license, scowled at Miranda's collarbone—nobody ever looked Miranda in the face—and after several deep breaths said, "You got proof of the new address? Power bill, phone bill, water bill, mail addressed to you?"

"My first power bill," Miranda said, sliding the envelope farther across the counter.

The official squinted at the address on the correspondence.

"Minokee? Does anybody still live in Minokee?" Then, over the shoulder again, "Freddie, is folks still livin' in Minokee?" Then, to Miranda, "You really moved to Minokee?"

"Yes, ma'am, I sure did."

"From where?"

"Miami."

A satisfied nod at Miranda's bodice buttons. *Explains a lot*, said the eyes. "Step over there in front of the blue screen," the official ordered.

Miranda wove her way across the room to stand in front of the screen and face the digital camera.

Minutes passed. Miranda's official approached the camera from the other side of the counter, carrying Miranda's papers, then stood looking about the room. "Ogilvy!" she shrieked. "Miriam Ogilvy!"

From three feet in front of the camera Miranda waved and smiled. "Right here. It's Miranda. Miranda Ogilvy."

"Whatever," said the official. "Look right here." She tapped a spot on the front of the camera. With her other hand she swatted at a fly trying to roost on the camera lens.

The fly buzzed straight at Miranda's face, Miranda reacted instinctively, and the result was a high-tech digital photograph of the top of Miranda's head with her two hands flailing above it like moose antlers.

"Crap," said the official when the new license rolled out of the laminator. She showed the moose photo to Miranda.

"It's better than the old one," Miranda said encouragingly.

The harried official looked at the photo and at the melting masses still waiting in the long, long, long line of customers.

"You're right," she said, handing Miranda the new license together with the supporting papers. "Have a nice day."

"Thank—" Miranda almost said.

"Next!" the woman blared as if nobody was standing right in front of her.

I guess nobody is, thought Miranda and murmured a "Thank you" that nobody heard.

4 THE LIBRARIAN

Herbert Lundstrom's wife, Hazel, often said of her husband, "He's short and bald with large pores, but he's so wonderful." And he was. He was kind, sympathetic, sweet natured, and helpful. In short, he was ill suited for civil service work, but the State of Florida had not yet discovered it, so he remained on the job. Miranda Ogilvy was blessed to be in his office a quarter-hour after leaving the DMV.

Lundstrom worked in Human Resources, and it was his joy to tell Miranda her new job at the Live Oak Public Library was waiting for her.

"I'm so glad to meet you in person, after all our correspondence and phone calls," Lundstrom said as he ushered Miranda into his cubicle. "It's not often we have an applicant with your credentials in a town this size. Miami's loss is Live Oak's gain, eh?"

"Actually, we met yesterday afternoon at Phyllis Ogilvy's memorial service," Miranda said pleasantly.

"We did?" Clearly Lundstrom had forgotten.

"But it's good to see you again," said Miranda, who had expected nothing else.

Leaning back in his faux leather chair, which Hazel had lovingly chosen for him from a very upscale office equipment catalog, Lundstrom made a tent with his fingers and smiled in Miranda's direction. "So, tell me, Mary—"

"Miranda."

"—right—tell me, how in the world did you acquire a house in Minokee? I was shocked to see your address. It's such a tiny community, they say nothing is ever available in real estate there unless somebody dies." He chuckled.

"Somebody died," said Miranda.

"Oh?" The chuckle became an uncertain smile.

"Phyllis Ogilvy? You were at her memorial service yesterday?"

"Oh! Oh, Phyllis, yes! Of course, yes. She was one of our civil service employees, you know."

"Yes, I know," said Miranda. "You're giving me her job."

"Pardon?"

"The librarian position here in Live Oak. That was Phyllis' old job. She was the librarian here since before I was born. But you already knew that." Miranda smiled.

Lundstrom smiled, too, but his eyes were blank. Apparently he knew nothing of the sort. They smiled at each other across his desk while his Birds of America clock, another gift from Hazel, chirped off several seconds.

Suddenly, Lundstrom surged to his feet and thrust his glad hand toward Miranda. "Well, it's great to have you with us. See Tom in Accounting to fill out the tax forms and such, and report to the library bright and early Monday morning."

Miranda bounced up and shook the proffered hand. "Thank you, Mr. Lundstrom. I look forward to the new assignment."

"Right you are. Good day, Michelle."

"It's Mi–, uh, good day, Mr. Lundstrom."

Miranda went to see Tom in Accounting, even though she knew that Tom in Accounting, naturally, would not really see her.

5 THE CASTOR BEAN

When the Little Cypress National Forest was established in the crook of Florida's elbow, there were a few logging roads and two short, narrow residential streets deep inside the forest. That was in the 1940s.

The dozen small homes clustered on adjacent Magnolia and Orchid Streets were the only structures permitted within the Little Cypress. They were grandfathered in, largely to save the money it would've cost to condemn the properties under eminent domain laws and pay off the resident families. Those two crooked streets and twelve rickety-looking wooden houses in the middle of the woods made up the miniscule community called Minokee.

"Minokee" was said to be a Seminole Native American word meaning "chock full of big, hungry reptiles." Experts disagreed on the exact translation. In any case, the forest around Minokee was not exactly a swamp, but a short jungle hike would take a person from the asphalt streets to the puddles, ponds and streams where alligators and cottonmouth water moccasins plied their toothy trade. On calm evenings the growls and grunts of mate-seeking bull 'gators carried all the way to the verandas of Minokee. It wasn't quite as romantic or exotic as hearing lions roar in the night across the Serengeti, but it was an excellent reminder that the Little Cypress National Forest had its own "king of the jungle."

And the king of Minokee's jungle was not warm, cute, lovable Simba.

Miranda Ogilvy was hired on Friday afternoon. She spent Saturday unpacking her few belongings and settling in to her late Aunt Phyllis' little old Minokee house. Sunday was going to be her day to rest up from relocating three hundred miles with less than a week's notice, following the sudden death of her aunt. On Monday morning, Miranda would report for duty as the newest librarian at the Live Oak Municipal Library.

Sunday morning found Miranda too excited to sleep, so the sun was not even up when Miranda slipped into the rubber flip-flops she kept by her front door. She wore nothing else but the extra-large SpongeBob Squarepants tee shirt in which she slept. After sharing her Miami apartment with two roommates in order to afford the rent, Miranda relished being alone now in her own house and not having to be dressed for society before leaving her bedroom.

She planned to retrieve the Sunday paper from the front yard and then spread it all over the living room while eating powdered doughnuts and drinking coffee right there in front of God and everybody—well, nobody—and that was the beauty of it! No one would tell her to get dressed, eat in the dining room, don't leave a mess, don't get the newspaper sections out of order. No one would say anything because no one was there but Miranda, in Miranda's very own, very small, very old, slightly weird, much appreciated, pokey Minokee house.

She parted the blinds beside the front door and peeked out into the gray morning. A twinge of pink touched the tops of the palm and live oak trees; the sun would crawl over the horizon soon. Too early for anyone to be up, surely. Too delicious that she could race out and snatch the paper off the lawn with no one the wiser. She smiled to herself, unlatched the front door, and scampered out onto the porch.

"Mornin', Miss Ogilvy!" shouted the old lady across the street.

Miranda squeaked and dove under the broad leaves of a tall plant.

"Mornin', neighbor," sang out another lady.

Miranda cleared her throat. "Morning, y'all," she called tentatively.

"You can stand up, dear, it's only us girls," came from another porch nearby.

Miranda pushed aside leaves the size of garbage can lids and reconnoitered. She could see an old lady with—was that a rifle?—across the street; another lady next door to Gun Lady, and two more on porches along Miranda's side of the street. Slowly she stood, picked up the Sunday newspaper, and stepped around the mammoth plant to the curlicued iron gate in her waist-high stone fence.

"Y'all up this early every day?" she asked.

"Magnolia Street coffee ritual," said the lady with—yes, it was definitely—a rifle. "Get yer cup and come on out. I'm Martha; that there's Bernice," she pointed over her shoulder, "and that's Wyneen and Charlotte." She gestured to Miranda's side of the street. "We met at the memorial service, but don't fret if ya don't remember ever'body yit."

Bernice spoke up from her rocker, "Mind yer bidness there, Martha. Ain't that them a'comin' right now?"

Martha whipped up a set of binoculars and focused down the road past Miranda. "Yep, 'at's them."

"That's who?" said Miranda, turning to look in the direction indicated. A huge dog and a half-naked man (maybe three-quarters naked!) were running—running! Directly at her.

Miranda squeaked, dove again under the broad-leaved plant, and squeezed herself into the tiniest possible ball, tucked against the inside of her low, stone, garden wall.

"It's a no-shirt day!" Martha crowed. The other ladies made sounds usually associated with double chocolate fudge cake under homemade whipped cream.

Miranda closed her eyes tightly and squatted, trying to pull her SpongeBob shirt down over her thighs, knees, ankles, and toes. No use. She could hear the whhp-whhp-whhp of the man's sneakers on the road, closer and closer and—

The women began shrieking.

"Mornin', Shep and Dave!"

"Mornin' Shep!"

"Good morning, Shepard!"

"Howdy, Shep and Dave!"

Miranda's heart lurched in her chest when a deep voice very near her fence responded with morning greetings to Martha, Bernice, Wyneen, and Charlotte. Miranda stopped breathing altogether when the same voice, inches away from her hiding place, whispered, "Why are you hiding under there? Are you not decent?"

Miranda didn't answer. She couldn't.

"It's okay. I absolutely cannot see you. Promise."

"H-how d-did y-you...?"

"How did I know you were in there?" There was a smile in his voice.

"Uh-huh."

"What's happenin', Martha?" Bernice called.

"Krausse is talkin' to the Ogilvy girl. Nuthin' to see. I'm goin' in," answered Martha. Her screen door creaked and whapped as she left her porch.

Within seconds, three other noisy screen doors testified that the ladies had returned to their houses.

"They're gone," Shep said to the plant. "You can come out."

"No, thank you," said Miranda shyly.

"Suit yourself. In answer to your question, Castor Bean Tree, you smell absolutely heavenly—which is highly unusual for castor beans, as any kid who ever took castor oil will attest. Therefore, I cleverly deduced that either this was a one-in-a-zillion castor bean tree, or a new neighbor has moved in on Magnolia Street. That would be you. I'm Shepard Krausse, by the way. And this is Dave."

The dog whuffed in greeting. Standing flatfooted on the road, Dave's head rested comfortably on the top of the stone fence, and he gazed with interest at the talking plant.

Miranda's hand protruded from between leaves and patted around until she found Shepard's hand resting on the fence. They shook hands. "I'm Miranda," she said.

Without releasing her hand, Shep bent at the waist and rested his forearms on top of the stone fence. Mister Friendly. "Some people think he's Shep and I'm Dave; I guess they think Shep should be a dog's name. But it's easy to tell us apart. Dave's smarter, but I'm cuter."

"Rrrrmf," said Dave.

"Okay, Dave's smarter and cuter, but I'm the one with the good personality."

"Rrrrmf."

"Okay, okay, Dave's smarter, cuter, and more personable, but I … uh … oh! I can play the piano!"

Dave whined.

"I didn't say I play well."

"Rrrrmf."

"Our house is directly behind yours," Shep said, now holding her hand between both of his. "We face Orchid Street. Your lot shares a back hedge with ours."

"Uh-huh," said Miranda, tugging on her hand.

He released her. "You're really lucky to get a house in Minokee, you know. People hardly ever sell here. My house belonged to my grandparents. Everybody in the neighborhood's been here since God was in Pampers."

"Uh-huh."

"You shoulda known the old termagant who used to live in your house. Boy, she was a fireball. Fearless Phyllis we called her. She would have fought the devil with a can opener—and probably woulda won. And boy, what a know-it-all. She had an answer for everything, and an opinion to go with it." Shep chuckled to himself. "Good old Fearless Phyllis. So, how'd you get this house, you lucky duck?"

"Aunt Fearless croaked," she said pointedly.

Shepard was momentarily silenced, suddenly conscious of how rude and callous his words must have sounded to a grieving niece.

Dave whuff-whuffed.

"Dave thinks I'm an idiot," Shep said.

"Uh-huh," said Miranda.

"Well, we won't keep you. Welcome to the neighborhood. Let's go, Dave." Shep and Dave moved away from the fence. As they jogged away, Shep spoke to the dog, "Why'n't ya tell me ta shut up, doofus?"

"Whuff," said Dave.

"Yeah, yeah," Shep responded.

Miranda raised herself onto her knees and looked between elephantine leaves at the departing pair. How often did no-shirt day come around? She'd had scarcely a glimpse of the man while she cowered beneath her leaf umbrella; it was only natural to wonder whether the muscles on his front were as impressive as the very well developed muscles she now observed on his back. She resolved to join the Magnolia Street ladies for coffee every morning from now on, but she would get dressed before coming outdoors in the future.

6 THE ALARM

Shepard Krausse worked nights. He exploited his hot-molasses baritone as host of a late-night radio program called Sheep Counters. His shtick was that his purpose in life was to serve the insomniacs whose conspiracy theories were keeping them awake. When the old trick of counting sheep didn't work, the sufferer could call in and commiserate with a shepherd—in this case, Shepard.

Yeah. Ha. Ha.

It was corny, but in rural north-central Florida the show was a staple and had a loyal following. Get it? Following? Sheep?

Well, it was what it was, and for Shep and Dave it was a living. Dave could come to work with his best friend, and Shep didn't have to cut his hair to work at a "real job" in the big city.

Of course, the silliest puns and the most regrettable jokes on the program were always attributed to Dave. Dave also served as purported researcher and all-around consultant on "the issues," which were whatever Shepard said they were.

This particular day was different in only one way: today Shep and Dave had talked to a castor bean tree, and they would never be the same. (Dave was totally smitten.) Who could have known that the dawn's routine after-work run would be a life changer?

Most days the pair worked their on-air shift from 11 p.m. to 3 a.m., commuted from Live Oak back home to Minokee, ran a few miles, then showered and collapsed into the deep sleep of the pure in heart. Today, Shepard had lain awake all day, hands behind his head, face toward the ceiling, debating with himself.

Despite his joking with Miranda about the foibles of Fearless Phyllis, Shep and his late neighbor, the elder Miss Ogilvy, had been on very friendly terms. She had worked days, and he had worked nights. Still, their ships had passed in the twilight from time to time, and even with, say, thirty years' difference in their ages (that's giving old Phyllis the benefit of significant doubt), they enjoyed one another's company.

Even when, as a child, Shepard had visited his grandparents' house—in which he now lived—he had never missed a chance to cross the two back yards to Phyllis' kitchen door. Phyllis had always greeted him warmly but very seriously. She was the first person in his life who had treated him like a responsible, self-sufficient human being with a good head on his shoulders. He was eight at the time.

Did he still have a good head on his shoulders? He wondered, blue eyes wide open as they had been for hours. Phyllis may have mentioned relatives in Miami. Shepard couldn't remember. He certainly didn't recall any prior knowledge that would have prepared him for Miranda Ogilvy, the transplanted, inheriting niece.

Assuming he was correct, that he had known nothing about Miranda until today, *how could he be...? Well, he couldn't, that's all. But then, why did he feel so positive that he, that she, that they...? Well, he couldn't be positive, could he? And wasn't he a grown man with a normal, productive, contented life? He couldn't suddenly be incomplete because he had crossed paths with a stranger today.*

Sure, he could.

No, he couldn't.

And what about Miranda? What would make him think that he impressed her as anything other than a consummate dolt? Nothing, that's what.

And so it went, round and round, hour after hour, and would have continued except that Dave, lying on the cool tile floor beside the bed as usual, suddenly raised his head and ears and whuffed. A second later, Shep heard someone enter through the back door.

"Sleep!" he whispered to Dave.

Dave dropped his chin onto his outstretched front paws and closed his eyes. Shepard rolled onto his side and curled into the fetal position under the covers. It was a stellar performance and did no good at all.

The bedroom door crashed back against the wall, shattering the quiet, and that was only the beginning.

"Get up, Goldilocks!" a man thundered from the doorway.

Shepard's only reaction was to yawn theatrically and turn over onto his back, eyes closed. Immediately Dave yawned theatrically and rolled over, lifting all four feet into the air, eyes closed.

"Everybody's a comedian," the man said without humor and with a pronounced Italian accent. "Quit playing and get outta da bed right now. I made lasagna, and by my grandfather's beard, you gonna eat it before we go. And we gonna leave on time. You late one more time, you gonna have to go out and find serious work!"

Eyes closed, Dave whined.

Shep translated, one eye open. "The lasagna, it's not vegetar--?"

"Not vegetarian," the man interrupted. "No, itsa not vegetarian, I learna my lesson." The man turned to leave the room, muttering over his shoulder, "I'ma waste my considerable, *considerable* talents on you ungrateful barbarians."

Shep sat up in bed and shouted down the hall, where the man had gone. "Hey, did you lay out my clothes?"

Dave rolled right side up, stood, and shook himself awake.

From the kitchen the man's voice rasped loudly, "Hangin' in the bathroom, Pretty Boy! Get a move on!"

"Thank you, Pietro," Shepard called in a syrupy sing-song.

"Whuff aruh," barked Dave.

. . . .

Less than thirty minutes had passed when Dave preceded Shepard into the kitchen. Shep took a seat at the dark, heavy wooden table that had been his grandmother's pride. He could have seen himself in the polished surface, but he didn't. Pietro set a plate of steaming lasagna between the utensils laid at Shep's place.

"Thank you," said Shep.

Dave sat, eyes bright, ears upright, and tail wagging, in the corner nearest the kitchen sink. A vinyl placemat and stainless steel dish of cool water occupied the corner tiles. Pietro set a stainless steel bowl of kibble topped with lasagna on the mat beside the water dish.

"Whuff aruh," barked Dave, but he didn't move from where he sat.

"Let'sa pray," said Pietro. Dave lowered his chin, Shep bowed his head, and Pietro intoned toward the ceiling, "For what we are about to receive, gracious Lord, make our selfish hearts truly grateful. May this food and your Holy Spirit fuel us to live for your glory. Amen."

"Amen," said Shep, then picked up his fork and began eating.

"Whuff," said Dave, then dove snoot-first into the food bowl.

Pietro brought a plate for himself and took a seat across the table from Shepard. Forks scraped, and mmm's of appreciation bespoke deliciousness, complimenting the cook. Moments later Shep swallowed a bite and cleared his throat.

"What?" said Pietro.

"Had a visitor waiting when I got back from my run this morning."

"And...?"

"In the house, sitting on the couch."

"You leave-a da house unlocked?"

"Wouldn't have mattered to this guy. Is there bread, please?"

Pietro's chair scraped. "Jiminy Christmas, I forgetta da oven!"

"Explains the charcoal smell."

Pietro yanked on an oven mitt and jerked a smoking pan of garlic bread from the oven. He slammed the oven door and dropped the pan in the sink. Removing his oven mitt, he resumed his seat at the table. "No, we don't-a got bread, Smarty Trousers. Now you quit da stallin' and tell me what da guy want in you house on you couch before da sun even come up good."

"Is there more sweet tea, please?"

"Talk, or you be wearin' all the sweet tea we got!" Nevertheless, Pietro retrieved a pitcher from the fridge and refilled his and Shep's glasses.

"Seems somebody's not a fan of the Shep and Dave show. I mean, they like Dave just fine, but they think I'm sharing too many personal opinions about things I know nothing about. The guy wasn't too specific, but I got the feeling he meant opinions about things that could hurt a certain governor's chances of becoming vice president of the United States."

Pietro slapped the tabletop. "I told you! I told you, you mother told you, you uncle told you, and now you gotta bad, bad people telling you. Stay outta politics! You got a show dat's number one with all the insomniacs and hillbillies and conspiracy loonies. You got friends and relatives who love you. You got a good life—even got a house in Minokee, and almost nobody got dat. You riska too much, talkin' about the governor. And you gotta no proof. You gonna get sued and lose all you money. Or worse, some bad guy gonna be waitin' for you some mornin' and you gonna lose you life! You gotta stop it now. Dis da last turkey in the straw, you gotta stop!"

"Yeah, I thought that's what you'd say," said Shep, munching the last bites of his lasagna. "The turkey part was a surprise, though. That's new."

Pietro put his elbows on the table and dropped his forehead into his hands. "You not gonna stop."

"Nope."

"You know, the ravings of one demented old lady ain't important enough to risk you life!"

"Phyllis was the least demented person I ever met, and she never raved. Ranted plenty, ranted like a street preacher sometimes, but she never raved. Phyllis was no lunatic. I know that as well as I know my own name."

"I tell you what I know," said Pietro. "I know Phyllis Ogilvy is dead. You thinka dat?"

"I think of that a lot. I wonder if Fearless Phyllis had a visitor in her house, on her couch, who wanted her to stop. Stop calling the talk shows. Stop writing letters to the editor. I wonder if someone stopped Phyllis."

"Iffa you think dat, you calla da police. You don'ta get involved and get stopped you own self."

Shepard rose, picked up his empty plate and dirty flatware, and carried them to the sink. "Long drive ahead of us. Don't wanna be late. Would you let Dave out in the back yard while I brush my teeth, please? Then we'll hit the road." Shep left the kitchen and headed to his bedroom and en suite bathroom.

Dave stood at the back door and looked over his shoulder at Pietro, who was placing the last dirty dishes in the sink.

"I'ma come, I'ma come, Dave. Gimme one minute." Then he shook his head and murmured, "He ain't gonna stop, you know. He talk to so many crazies, he gone crazy his own self."

"Whupff," said Dave.

7 THE DEEJAY

Several hours later, inside Studio B of Live Oak's all-talk radio station, Shepard, wearing headphones, sat at the mixing board with a telephone on his right and a digital sound effects console on his left. A microphone in an anti-vibration mount hung before his face, protected by a pop filter that looked like an embroidery hoop inside a scrap of pantyhose.

The mixing board had "pots," or sound level controls, for dozens of inputs—everything from the telephone to the computer playing music and commercials to the live mic that would carry Shepard's basso profundo over the airwaves.

The program lineup appeared on a computer screen mounted level with and in front of Shepard's right shoulder, when Shep was seated. A second control room boasted equipment from which he could broadcast standing, if he chose to do so.

Dave dozed on the floor near Shepard's rolling chair. Outside the soundproof control room, Pietro was answering phones and taking information from callers. Pietro could watch Shep through the control room's picture window—which was angled to prevent unwanted sound bouncing back into the mic. Shep, in his ever-present sunglasses, never turned his face toward the window.

Shep listened on his headphones, both hands poised on the mixing board, as the final seconds of a pre-recorded commercial ticked by. In his headphones, over the muted sound of the commercial, an appealing digital female voice intoned, "four...three...two."

Shepard pushed up the pot for his mic and pulled down the pot for the commercial, smoothly taking back the helm of his sheep-counting ship.

"Well, there's a full moon tonight, sheep counters, and you know what that means. That's right, the crazies are out. Give me a call at 877-555-S-H-E-P and tell me what the loons in your neck of the woods are up to tonight. This is Shepard Krausse, and you're listening to Sheep Counters with Shep and Dave on eighty-three point nine, WLOK-FM in Live Oak."

While his voice rolled on, smooth as dark chocolate, he could hear Pietro's voice in his headphones, advising Shep of a waiting caller.

Shep raised the telephone pot on his mixing board as he spoke into the mic. "Good evening, fellow sheep counter. You're on the air. Do you have a full moon story for us?"

"Boy howdy! I shore do," a man replied.

"Am I correct that we're talking with Earl from Uhumpka?" said Shep.

" 'At's me."

"And what's your story, Earl?"

"Well, me and my cousin Walter was coon huntin' out in the Little Cypress during a full moon about two years ago, and we definitely saw a Chupacabra. I kid you not, we was no more'n fifty yards from it. It 'uz moving east to west through the swamp, an' our coon dogs like ta went nutso...."

And on he went, occasionally prompted with a question from Shep, who encouraged and reinforced the caller at every opportunity. The Chupacabra—sometimes called the Sasquatch of South America—was standard fare for superstitious, sleep-deprived, liquor-swilling sheep counters.

The night progressed through callers' stories of UFO sightings and alien abductions, ghosts of murder victims, black helicopters, spy satellites, government monitoring of telephone communications, and more. Full moon. No caller too wacky, no story too improbable for Sheep Counters.

Shep was everyone's buddy, approving and affectionate and ready to back 'em up when they faced detractors. From time to time, callers asked for Dave's opinion. Shep relayed each question, Dave whuffed a response, and Shep translated Dave's answer for the members of the audience who might not speak canine.

Shep was commenting on a caller's theory that cable television providers were looking into the living rooms of their subscribers. "They could do it, sure. No question they could be watching us while we're watching them. But why would they want to? I mean, what are they going to see? The bottoms of our feet propped up in our recliners? Uncle Ned drinking beer in his undershorts? Aunt Myrtle asleep in her chair with her mouth open and her teeth in her lap?"

"So, you're sayin' 'Don't worry about it'?" asked the caller.

"Well, here's the thing," Shep replied. "If you come home and your wife is gyrating naked in front of the television set—without benefit of an exercise video—that would be the time to worry whether the guys at the cable company are watching you. Until then, I wouldn't sweat it. Have a great night. Thanks for calling."

Shep punched the next button on the incoming phone lines. "Welcome, sheep counter, you're on the air."

"Hello, Shep and Dave. This is Robert calling from High Springs."

"Welcome, Robert. What do you have for us?"

"Well, I been following the papers and the TV news, and I'm getting some confused messages about this construction bidding thing in Tallahassee. Don't seem like anybody's got a straight answer for anything. I was just wonderin' if you could sort of boil it down into simple language for me. What exactly is goin' on, and is it really important or it is a smoke screen to keep us from findin' out about somethin' worse?"

"Wow, Robert, that's a fantastic question. You hit the nail right on the head. Nobody is going to give us a straight answer on this thing because if they do, we will see clearly that nearly everybody involved is guilty of something. Some have broken the law—and profited by it at the expense of us, the taxpayers—and some have hidden the crimes of others."

"I don't doubt it," agreed Robert. "Just exactly what crimes are we talkin' about this time, Shep?"

"Robert, the law says that before the State of Florida hires a company to build a school or a police station or a road, the State must publish a description of the project and allow qualified construction companies to send in a sealed bid.

"The company that meets all the requirements of the bid and quotes the lowest price gets the job. In theory, the building gets built for the least possible cost to the taxpayers."

"What does it mean 'sealed' bids?" asked Robert.

"Just like you would seal an envelope so nobody knows what's inside, the bids are 'sealed' so that no construction company knows what any other construction company is bidding. Theoretically, if you knew what your competitor was bidding, you could just bid a dollar lower than his quote, and you'd get the job."

Pietro spoke into Shepard's ear via the headphones. "Don't-a say too much! You haven't gone too far yet! Don't-a say—"

Shep cut off the feed to the headphones.

Outside the slanted window Pietro threw papers into the air in frustration.

"Is that what's happenin'?" Robert was asking. "Somebody's leaking the bids so their cronies can bid lower?"

"You got it," Shep said. "Some people think it's strange that over the past five years, more than half of the construction bids have been won—by a narrow margin, I might add—by three companies. Some people are saying that if you check the corporate records, you'll find all three companies owned by the same person. Some people believe the owner of the three companies has been given inside information by someone in Tallahassee, so that he could win the bids."

Robert argued that if the bids were lower as a result of the leaks, the State was actually getting a better deal. Projects were being built for even less than the lowest sealed bid would have been.

"Not a bad philosophy," said Shep, "except that the three winning companies ended up billing the State for much, much more than they quoted as the cost of the project. They've got all kinds of excuses, of course. But some people think those low bids were not worth the paper they were written on. The construction company had no intention of building the project for the low price they put in their bid. That's fraud. That's stealing from us taxpayers. That's unfair to the competing, honest construction companies. That's the crime, Robert."

"Dang!" Robert sighed. "Who's leaking the information? There can't be that many people in the bureaucracy who would have access to the sealed bid information. And the one person who controls all three questionable construction companies – well, heck we don't have to name names here, but everybody knows who we're talkin' about. How can they get away with it? We know they're doing it! Why hasn't somebody been arrested? Why isn't somebody in prison?"

Pietro was now pounding on the control room door and giving Shepard threatening looks through the control room window.

"Robert, the man who owns these companies is making someone in state government very wealthy. And that someone is high enough up the food chain that nobody will ever be convicted of this particular crime while that government official remains in office.

"If you find out who that government official is, Robert, please don't tell anybody. People who have tried to identify that person and put a stop to this thing, well, those people have disappeared.

"And that's all our time for tonight, sheep counters. Thanks for calling. Have a great night."

Shep potted down the telephone input and cued up his theme music as he spoke into his mic. "You've been listening to Sheep Counters with Shep and Dave on eighty-three point nine, WLOK-FM in Live Oak. Join us again tomorrow night at eleven. Until then, sweet dreams."

He potted the mic down and the theme music up. He rolled backward across the control room in his chair. Pietro practically fell through the door when Shep swung it open.

"Are you happy now?" asked Pietro, straightening to his full height. "You probably killed all of us." He said it in the same way he might have said, "We'll probably have to stop for gas."

Shepard ignored him. "C'mon, Dave. Let's go home."

The three of them walked out of the station, got into the car Pietro drove, and rode in silence for fifteen minutes.

"I'm going to the store tomorrow," Pietro said at last. No point in discussing the angry criminals who were probably at this very moment planning Shepard's assassination.

"We need shower gel," said Shep. No point in assuring Pietro they were in no danger. They both knew better.

"Again! That stuff's expensive!"

"Dave likes it."

"Dave! What's he do, drink it?!"

"We have to take a shower every day. My aroma gets awfully manly after a run in this heat, y'know."

"Fine, you have to shower every day. It'sa not good for Dave, though. Dogs can get dry skin if they get a bath too often. Especially wit' espensive shower gel."

"Oh, that reminds me: we need another bottle of that moisturizing conditioner," inserted Shep.

"Whuff!" said Dave from the back seat.

"Jiminy Christmas," said Pietro.

8 THE LIBRARY

Annabelle Sherwood tossed her voluminous red curls back over her shoulder with practiced grace and batted her false eyelashes at the man who had greeted her. Sure, old Mr. Brazleton could not see well enough to appreciate the stunning cleavage Annabelle displayed in her low-cut silk blouse, but he was still male and capable of making out her hourglass silhouette. He could smell her costly designer perfume with heavy musk undertones (Annabelle would slather herself with undiluted pheromones if it were possible).

But Annabelle knew her only reward from Mr. Brazleton would be his toothless, admiring grin. He had neither the money nor the working plumbing to take Annabelle out for lunch, much less for an evening—or night—on the town.

Good thing about a small town like Live Oak: Annabelle knew the financial and marital status of every man who entered her library. She knew how to get the most from every one, and she wasted no time on the poor, the puny, the perverted, or the Happily Married.

Miranda Ogilvy, the new librarian, had observed Annabelle in action for only a day and a half, and already Miranda was in awe of (and a little disgusted by) her curvy coworker.

When the marvelous Annabelle crooned greetings at old Mr. Brazleton in her most seductive siren's voice, Miranda was surprised at first. Brazleton was not the type Annabelle usually targeted. Then Annabelle winked at Miranda and returned Brazleton's smile with apparent sincerity. Annabelle was being kind to the lonely octogenarian, in Annabelle's way.

"That was sweet," Miranda told Annabelle when Brazleton doddered out the front door.

"Yeah," Annabelle sighed. Then she shrugged it off. "He's harmless, y'know? Besides, it's been a slow day and I can always benefit from a bit of practice."

"You are a really good person, Annabelle," Miranda said.

"Okay, don't ever let anybody hear you say that. You could ruin my reputation. Shelve these for me?" Annabelle hefted a stack of returned books onto a rolling cart and nudged the cart toward Miranda.

"Of course." Miranda expected nothing else. Why should the swan do grunt work when the ugly duckling was at hand? Besides, even if Miranda stood alongside Annabelle at the check-in counter, patrons would form a line in front of Annabelle and never notice Miranda's existence. Thus, Annabelle spent most of the day on display at the front desk, while Miranda disappeared into the stacks.

. . . .

Outside the library, Pietro wheeled into the parking space closest to the front door. He let the motor and air conditioner run while he turned toward Shepard, who was unbuckling his seat belt.

"I can go in alone," Pietro insisted. "Why deal with the man-eater if you don'ta got to? I can return dese and pick up the ones from the Hold shelf. Gimme you card." Pietro reached for a bulging floral tote bag resting by Shep's feet.

Shep snatched the bag from Pietro's reach. "I'll check in while you check out. We'll finish in half the time, and we won't be late for work."

"Nnnnooo," Pietro whined. "I don'ta like doin' this. Is not honest. Is denigrate my manhood. Is spoil my image witha da ladies."

"Oh, hush," said Shep and opened the passenger door. "Leave the AC on for Dave. We'll be just a minute, Dave."

From the back seat Dave whuffed and lay down to wait.

Pietro sighed dramatically, then opened the car door. "Show time," he said to himself as he left the driver's seat.

He rounded the hood of the car and joined Shep, who was standing beside the passenger door, holding the conspicuous, flowery tote bag. Pietro held out his left elbow, Shep placed his right hand on his friend's arm, and they walked toward the library steps together.

Miranda returned to the front desk to collect more books for shelving. Annabelle touched her shoulder and pointed outside the building's glass facade. Two attractive men climbed the steps, arm in arm, dressed like fashion models, wearing sunglasses. The bearded one had long platinum hair spreading across his wide shoulders and down his back. The other was dark, clean-shaven, small-boned, and wore Euro-style half boots with his silk slacks. The big, hairy one could have been mistaken for a Viking warrior if he hadn't been carrying a huge purse with pink flowers on it. Something familiar niggled just beyond Miranda's conscious memory.

"It's them," Annabelle whispered.

"It's whom?"

"The local queer contingent." Annabelle's shoulders rose and fell in an exaggerated sigh. "Such a tragic waste."

The two women watched the men climb the steps and enter the glass doors. Inside the doors, the dark one pointed the golden one toward the women, and the dark one paced toward the Hold shelves across the lobby. The Viking queen approached the counter.

Miranda heard, "Goin' on break," and Annabelle disappeared.

Miranda put on the Smile of the Professional Librarian and waited to be ignored by the newcomer.

Black glasses seemed to stare through her, exactly as she expected, when the man stopped in front of her and clumped his large purse onto the counter. He sniffed the air. He leaned closer to Miranda and sniffed again. He stood tall and broke into the grin children wear on Christmas morning.

"Castor Bean!?" he guessed.

"Mr. Krausse?" she exhaled in disbelief.

"What are you doing here?" they both asked at once, then chuckled.

"I work here," she said.

"Of course. You would," he said.

"Just like Aunt Phyllis!" they said together, and she laughed.

"And you?" asked Miranda.

"Got books to check in," Shep answered. He stacked the books from the tote bag onto the counter. "Almost didn't know you with your clothes on," he teased.

"I had clothes on the last time. And you said you couldn't see me!"

"Didn't. You still smell the same, though. I was confused there for a second with what's-her-name's perfume still in the air, but I'd know your scent anywhere."

Miranda began scanning the books and placing them on a re-shelving cart. "You prefer audio books."

"Yeah. Long commute to work. We listen to books in the car."

Miranda nodded. "I had an even longer commute in Miami than I have here. My aunt used to send me a new foreign language course for my birthday every year. I've learned Spanish, French, German, and Italian in the traffic on South Dixie Highway."

He laughed. In German, he said, "We'll have to get together and talk some time."

She answered in French, "Are you trying to lure me to your bachelor pad?"

In Italian, he asked, "Could you be lured so easily, signorina?"

"I don't *play* hard to get," was her reply in Spanish. "I *am* hard to get. Impossible, practically." Then she spoiled her feigned hauteur with a giggle.

He chuckled, enjoying the game.

Miranda switched to English. "Your accent is better than mine. I'm guessing you didn't learn those languages in your car."

"Boarding school in Switzerland. Survival skills, really. We had to speak French to the professor of humanities, Italian to the chef, Spanish to the riding instructor, and German to the science teacher. The curse of the rich kid." His open smile and self-deprecating manner were endearing.

"Sounds miserable," she joked. "I'm so glad you escaped with your life." She turned to place the last of his books onto the re-shelving cart. "I see you read a lot of Dean Koontz novels."

"Dave loves the ones with dogs, especially dogs that are smarter than humans."

"So these are really Dave's books."

"Busted. He's waiting in the car."

"Well, tell him I like Dean Koontz, too. Has Dave read the book written by Koontz's dog, Trixie?"

Shepard faked dire alarm and faux-whispered, "Oh, heavens! He had such a crush on her! Don't mention that book in front of Dave! He didn't get out of bed for two days when Trixie passed away."

"I checked outta da books from the holding shelf," announced Pietro, plunking four audio books onto the counter alongside the flowered bag. In the same instant, an avalanche of books tumbled from the re-shelving cart to the floor with a clatter. When Pietro raised his eyes from his books to where Miranda had been standing, she was gone.

She had dropped to her hands and knees, scrambling after fallen audio books—some of the packages had popped open, spinning silver discs in all directions.

"Pietro, this is Miranda. Miranda, this is my old friend, Pietro. He and I actually went to boarding school together. Pietro, Miranda just moved into Phyllis' house."

Pietro, seeing no one, but hearing noises, leaned over the counter to where he glimpsed a bit of Miranda's backside. *"Ciao, bella!"* he said, admiring the parts he could see.

"Enchanté," called Miranda from the floor. Pietro loaded the new books into the flowery tote bag and placed it in Shepard's hand.

"We need-a to go, sweetheart," Pietro said loudly, glancing about in search of Annabelle.

"Yes, dear," Shep boomed, then said quietly in Miranda's direction, "It was great talking with you, Bean. See ya around."

"Yeah, see ya," called Miranda from the floor, and waved one hand above the counter's edge.

Annabelle sashayed to the counter just as Miranda stood up with books and discs in her arms. Annabelle did not reach to help, of course. Instead she watched the two men walking arm-in-arm down the steps toward the parking lot. "Such a waste," she said with a sigh.

9 THE CONSPIRACY

Governor Reginald Jackson Montgomery looked like a man who could be president someday: designer hairstyle, golden Florida tan, photogenic blue eyes, blinding white smile, leading-man looks, billionaire wardrobe. Reginald could actually trace his family line back to the first governor of Florida, Andrew Jackson—who, himself, had gone on to become president.

Unlike Andrew Jackson, Reginald Jackson Montgomery did not plan to become president. Frankly, it was too much stress and too much danger, with too little fun and way too little privacy. No, Reginald was going to be vice president, which would entail almost as many photo ops, but fewer sleepless nights on the brink of global catastrophes.

There was one way in which Reginald emulated his ancestor, Andrew: they were both foul-mouthed and corrupt. Allegedly corrupt in Reggie's case, since he had avoided arrest, indictment, or conviction thus far.

Of course, Reginald was not stupid. In this era of sound bites, ubiquitous cameras, and long-range microphones, Reginald kept his bad language private. Andrew had taken no such precautions with his verbiage back in the 19th century, and he had suffered for it. Reginald and his image-advisers had taken that lesson to heart.

Following a prestigious charity luncheon at a swank Tallahassee hotel, Reginald left his security detail outside the men's room door and, being assured the room was clear, ducked in for a few moments of solitude. He touched up his perfect hair, carefully flicking a few strands so they drooped toward his eyebrow in calculated disarray. He cultivated the image of a hardworking servant of the people, showing the strain of his selfless devotion to duty.

Women who thronged to shake his hand as he left the hotel in a few minutes would have the urge to smooth his hair; he would remind them of an adorable little boy in need of their mothering. His image consultant had coached him specifically on the hair trick, and he enjoyed using it.

The restroom door squeaked just as Reginald was leaning closer to the mirror to examine what surely could not be a gray hair. Reginald turned with rehearsed, regal posture to see who dared to enter. It was the man who had been an uninvited visitor to Shepard Krausse's living room earlier in the week. Reginald went back to studying his hair in the mirror.

"Make it quick," the governor said. "I want to get out of the hotel and into my limo before the afternoon thunderstorm opens up on us."

The henchman's haircut was imperfect, his teeth were yellow, his suit was off the rack at a men's clothing warehouse. He didn't have Paul Newman blue eyes. His eyes were an eerie gray so otherworldly that people were chilled by them and remembered them. Sometimes he didn't want to be remembered, so he did what he had to do to make it so. "Saw your nephew," he said.

"What did you think?"

"Impossible to tell. He may have the pictures and he may not. He could be just blowing smoke to keep the late-night radio nuts happy."

"Is he going to keep on blowing this smoke?" asked the governor, turning from the mirror to look into the gray eyes.

The henchman shrugged.

"Of course he will," Reginald said. "He was a good kid, but he's grown up too much like his grandparents: stubborn, self-righteous, and short-sighted. Shep just won't look at the bigger picture."

"At least he's not naming names," the henchman said. "He's given enough hints that everybody knows who the builder probably is, but I don't see anybody pointing fingers at particular government employees."

"Well, see that they don't! If anybody even whispers the name of anyone on my staff, you stop it cold. My plans are right on track for that vice presidential nomination, and nothing—no rumor, no scandal, no pictures in the paper— nothing can be allowed to connect me with Shepard Krausse's conspiracy fairy tale. You make sure of it. I'm paying you well, and I'll be holding you personally responsible."

The henchman nodded. "I plan to be proactive. Can't sit around hoping that old Audubon lady didn't have the proof she claimed. Could be she passed it along to Krausse and he's just waiting for the right time to spring it. Big ratings. Local hero. Y'know?"

The governor turned and washed his hands at the sink. He thought while he crossed to the towel dispenser and dried off. "You're right. I need Shepard to realize there will be serious consequences if he keeps stirring the pot on this bid-fixing thing. Do whatever you have to do to get his attention—just don't kill anybody this time!"

"How about the dog? Krausse sets a lotta store by that dog," said the henchman.

"You can do anything you like with that vicious mongrel," Reginald told him, and the governor left the room.

The henchman would not emerge until the governor's motorcade had left the hotel.

10 THE SNAKE

The Magnolia Street porch ladies, now increased by a factor of one, carried on the tradition of coffee sipped in front-porch rocking chairs in the misty, gray-green dawn. What got their hearts started each day was not the caffeine in the coffee, however. It was the whhp-whhp-whhp of sneakers on asphalt and the cheery greeting for each lady in turn from a passing Adonis.

Miranda sometimes felt that bibs would make perfect gifts for her fellow Shep-worshipers, so that their drool wouldn't damage their clothing. She made a mental note to Google some patterns and construct the bibs herself, maybe even embroidering them with each lady's name for a personal touch.

In Florida there are two seasons: wet season and dry season. June 1 through December 1 was the wet season. July steamed in the mornings and poured in the afternoons. Hanging laundry outside to dry became a calculated risk, and more than one set of bed linens got an unscheduled rinse in rainwater when its owner lost the race with a fast-moving cloudburst. Miranda was saving up for an electric clothes dryer.

On this particular July morning, Miranda had taken a break from completing the daily crossword puzzle—in ink, a secret source of pride for her—and she was perusing the classified ads for used appliances. Beside her on a fern stand was her mug of coffee.

At any moment, Martha would raise the alarm and all the ladies would sit forward for the best possible view of the Shep and Dave Parade. After her morning fix of beefcake, Miranda would shower, dress, and drive into Live Oak for a quiet day in the library.

"Here they come!" Martha announced, looking through her binoculars. Then with new alarm in her voice she cried, "Holy mother of pearl! Rattler! Rattler in the road!"

"Shoot it, Martha!" Bernice shrieked.

"Bernice, ya idjit! This pea shooter is fine for rabbits in the front yard, but it won't make a dent in a monster that size from this distance!"

"Can't they just go around it?" called Wyneen.

"Don't seem like they see it!" Charlotte said. "Looks like they'll run right up on it before they even know it's there!"

In the distance Shep and Dave loped toward them at an easy, regular pace. They didn't appear to angle left or right to avoid the dangerous reptile lying full-length across their path.

The snake was aware of them, however, no doubt sensing the vibration of the asphalt as they drew closer. Six feet of diamond-backed reptile began coiling in on itself in the road, head raised and tongue flicking toward the unwary man and his dog.

Miranda realized that she was standing at her gate, unaware that she had even risen from the rocking chair on the porch. She stared in horror at the snake. Two sounds assaulted her simultaneously: the whhp-whhp-whhp of running shoes and the warning rattle of the serpent's tail.

A hand touched Miranda's shoulder, and she screamed. She hadn't seen Martha cross the street to stand beside her.

"Phyllis kept a twelve-gauge in the hall closet. Is it still there?" said Martha.

Miranda gasped and mentally raced through the house recalling what Phyllis had left and where. "Yes!" she cried, and sprinted into the house.

Miranda threw open the hall closet, fumbled in the dark for the heavy shotgun and hauled it toward the light.

Outside, a dog began barking. The Magnolia Street ladies screeched in alarm. Miranda knocked shoe boxes and photo albums off the closet shelf and found a box of twelve-gauge shotgun shells.

She was already running through the front door and across the porch as she wrested two shells from the box, dropping the rest behind her without a second look.

In the street, Dave and the snake were only a few yards apart. Dave had blocked Shep's forward motion with his own shaggy flank.

Miranda broke open the shotgun over her forearm as she hurried through the low iron gate held open by Martha.

Shep pulled at Dave's bandanna and shouted "Leave it!" and "Back! Dave, back!" But Dave and the snake were battle-crazed and poised to attack.

Slamming shells into the two barrels, Miranda snapped the gun closed at the same time she was raising it to her shoulder.

"Get back, Shepard!" Miranda shrieked, then BAH-BOOM both barrels of the twelve-gauge spat fire and metal. The rattler's head bloomed into a cloud of red mist as big as a car tire. Its headless body writhed and then was still.

Miranda was catapulted backward two steps by the recoil of the gun, which seemed far too heavy to her in the aftermath. She let it droop at her side and leaned against her stone fence.

Shep was on his knees in the road, running his hands over Dave's forelegs and chest, head and belly.

"Did it get him?" Martha asked pragmatically, walking up to Shepard while looking intently at the dog.

"No, but it sure could have. Could've got us both," exhaled Shep. "I didn't even know it was there until Dave jumped in front of me. Nearly knocked me down, but he stopped me." He ruffled the dog's neck fur. "You stopped me, didn't ya, buddy. Good dog! Good dog."

Then Shep stood and turned in the direction of Miranda's house. Putting one hand on the dog's back, he said, "Let's go say thanks to Annie Oakley for saving our lives, eh?"

Martha sent a knowing smile and a wink in Miranda's direction then moved off to return home. "I'm gonna collect that skin afore some stupid car runs over it and ruins it," she called over her shoulder.

"Yewchh!" Miranda said, shuddering. She stared at the headless corpse for a second, then was distracted by the man coming at her. The closer he came, the higher she had to raise her chin to look up into his face. She saw herself twice-reflected in his sunglasses.

She was still waiting for him to speak when he grasped her arms just above her elbows and simply lifted her off the ground and planted a quick, hard kiss on her lips. He followed it with a longer, softer kiss, then lowered her until her toes touched the ground. He still trapped her close, his arms now circling her waist. "Thank you, Castor Bean," he whispered.

"Uh-huh." She thought she might faint, but then she might miss something,

"Tell me, where did you get an elephant gun at this hour of the day?" he said, chuckling.

"Closet," she sighed, trying to determine the color of his eyes behind the opaque glasses.

He rested his forehead against hers and nuzzled her nose with his own. He dislodged her black-rimmed spectacles, then gently re-settled them on her upraised face.

"You're wearing glasses," he said.

"I'm blind as a bat."

"Are you really?"

"Uh-huh."

"Y'know, I have a lot of blind friends. Maybe we know some of the same people."

What would be the odds of that? she thought. *He's larger than life, and I'm not sure I even exist!* Aloud, she told him, "Pretty sure we don't have the same circle of friends. I know I don't have any 'blind friends.' "

"You have me," he said, and kissed her forehead.

Miranda watched her dual reflection become smaller in the mirrored lenses of his glasses as he stepped back from her.

She leaned, limp and wide-eyed, against her stone fence. Her eyes focused straight ahead, scarcely even blinking. Her arms hung slack at her sides—the right hand still holding the empty shotgun, its muzzle dangling toward the ground.

Miranda licked her lips and tried again to see his eyes. All she could see was his smile as he backed away then turned and jogged on his way, Dave padding close alongside.

Miranda was amazed that she remained standing when every cell in her body had melted like hot wax. Some monumental knowledge was tapping at the edge of her brain, but it slipped off the molten wax every time she tried to reach it. *What did he say?*

Miranda didn't see or hear Martha approach, and when Martha took the shotgun, Miranda screamed.

"Good to know you're still in there," Martha said and chuckled. Miranda turned to look at her friend with more confusion than recognition. "I'll stick this back in the closet fer ya," Martha said, taking Miranda's elbow and turning her around to return to the house. "You need to get showered and dressed and off to work, now. I suggest cold water. Help ya git some a' yer wits a-workin' agin."

"Uh-huh," breathed Miranda, moving like a sleepwalker toward the house. Martha followed her, carrying Phyllis' old weapon.

11 THE WARNING

Miranda was still in a mild state of shock when she arrived for work at the library two and a half hours later. She locked her purse in her cubicle's bottom file drawer, straightened her calf-length skirt, and smoothed the sides of her hair, which hung in a plain, thick braid down her back. With one finger she shoved her eyeglasses up her nose, then she snagged the nearest cart of books and trundled out to lose herself in the stacks for most of the morning.

Annabelle did enough talking for three women, making Miranda's daylong silence a non-issue. Only once did Miranda rouse herself to conversation, when there were no patrons near enough to hear.

"Annabelle, are you absolutely sure Shepard Krausse is a homosexual?" she whispered.

Annabelle could have been heard for blocks as she laughed out loud then responded, "Honey chile, not to brag or anything, but I can make a dead dude stand up and whistle Dixie, y'know what I mean? But that guy! Never even gave me a second look. I'm not sure he ever gave me a first look, actually. Sweetie, he is definitely playing for the other team. Take my word for it!"

"But," Miranda shuffled her thoughts and tried again, "I didn't realize... Did you know Mr. Krausse is blind? I mean, really and truly blind!"

Annabelle was unfazed. "Then he's a blind homo. And really, nothin' would surprise me. Queer in one way, queer in a lotta ways. Know what I mean?"

"Mmm," murmured Miranda and returned to her books.

....

That evening after work, Miranda had just taken a frozen dinner out of the microwave when the ancient screen door on her front porch rattled thunderously. When she emerged from the kitchen to approach the front door, she saw a tall, elegantly dressed lady waiting imperiously beyond the screen.

The lady commented, "There appears to be nobody home."

"I'm right here," Miranda responded from the opposite side of the screen door. Their faces were separated by mere inches, but Miranda had to look up to meet the blue eyes glaring from above a patrician nose and disapproving lips.

"Can I help you?" asked Miranda without opening the screen door.

"You can invite me inside, young woman. I do not conduct family business on the front porch for the amusement of the neighborhood gossips," the lady answered, in cultured, confident tones.

"Family business?"

The woman simply stared, refusing to say another word until her conditions were met. Miranda opened the screen door and gestured toward her (late) Aunt Phyllis' sagging couch. "Please, won't you come in and sit down? I'm Miranda Ogilvy. I don't believe we've met."

"We have not. Nor would we be likely to if we did not have a mutual—not 'connection,' no—a mutual acquaintance." The woman looked at the couch as if it must surely harbor fleas. "I'll stand, thank you. I am Hermione Montgomery-Krausse. My son, Shepard, lives in the property adjoining this one, to the rear."

Delight lit Miranda's face. Impulsively she grasped the lady's gloved hand in both of hers. "You're Shepard's mother! I am so happy to meet you, Mrs. Krausse!"

"It's 'Montgomery hyphen Krausse,' Miss Ogilvy, and I should like to reclaim my hand now, if you please."

Miranda released the hand and almost bowed before this silver-haired, strikingly handsome woman. What was that scent? *Parfum de Paris?* Old money? Probably both, she decided. And who wore gloves these days? Besides Queen Elizabeth.

"Would you care for coffee or tea, Mrs. Montgomery-Krausse?" Miranda gestured to the dining room table and chairs.

Mrs. Montgomery-Krausse evaluated the dining furniture. Scarred, scratched, old, but good solid oak and well polished. No fleas. She could sit there. "Tea would be very nice," she said, moving to the table.

At a noise from the porch, Miranda turned to see a man in chauffeur's livery standing outside the door. She was about to invite him to wait inside and perhaps have refreshment, but before Miranda could speak, Lady Gotbucks intervened.

"My man will wait in the car. I won't be long."

"Yes, ma'am," said Miranda, and whispered, "Sorry," to the man outside. "I'll get the tea." Miranda disappeared into the kitchen.

As soon as Miranda left, Hermione waved a gloved hand, and the chauffeur silently entered the house, disappearing into the hallway beyond the living room. An instant later the man left as quietly as he had come, and he was carrying something. By the time Miranda returned with a tea tray, the chauffeur and his burden were gone.

Miranda poured tea and offered cream, sweetener, and lemon, without saying a word. When they had been served, she sat and focused on her guest. "You said something about family business?"

"What do you know about Shepard's family?" asked Mrs. Montgomery-Krausse.

"I know that his grandparents, Mr. and Mrs. Krausse, owned the house behind my Aunt Phyllis' house for many years." She gestured toward the house at the rear of the property.

"I am speaking of the Montgomery family."

"Oh." Miranda had nothing further to offer.

"Montgomery County, Montgomery Memorial Hospital, Montgomery Boulevard, *Governor* Montgomery? Is any of this ringing a bell?"

"Wow! Gosh." Miranda was trying to place all the references, but she was so new to the area that only one name was familiar. "Are you actually related to the governor of Florida?"

"Governor Reginald Montgomery is my brother," the older woman said. Then she made a very great point of adding, "And he is Shepard's uncle."

"Wow," Miranda whispered.

"Presumably Shepard has not told you, but he has a law degree from a prestigious Ivy League university. With his connections, he will be quite the rising star politically in this county, in this state, and hopefully on a national level. We are simply waiting for him to finish playing with his little radio program and his 'Old-Florida-living' phase—which is what *this* is." She gestured toward the house at the rear and then circled a hand to indicate Minokee in general.

Hermione Montgomery-Krausse pierced Miranda with her icy blue eyes and machine-gunned words at her. "Shepard is a direct descendant of a governor of Florida and a president of the United States. Shepard's uncle will in all likelihood become the next vice president of our nation.

"Shepard Montgomery Krausse is not just an eligible bachelor with money, Miss Ogilvy. He has been groomed from birth to be what passes for royalty in this country. Indeed, his physical disability only serves to make him even more charismatic and heroic than he would be normally."

Miranda said nothing as Hermione left her tea unfinished and rose to her impressive height. She looked down on Miranda as if from Olympus.

"That is who Shepard Montgomery Krausse is, Miss Ogilvy. Who, may I ask, are you?"

Miranda rose slowly to her feet and looked down, smoothing her skirt, before she looked up and returned Hermione's gaze.

"I'm nobody."

"Exactly," said Hermione. "In spite of your background, you seem to be of adequate intelligence to comprehend my message, are you not?"

"I understand you," said Miranda. "You completely misunderstand me, however. I am not pursuing your son, Mrs. Montgomery-Krausse. I hope someday to marry a man who sees me as no one else does and who loves me as no one else ever will. I haven't met that man yet, but I hope to. And when I do, I hope he and I will work together, play together, and raise a happy, healthy family together.

"I don't want to own the county, or control the state, or rule the world. And as long as I have the basic necessities of life, I am not interested in scads of money."

"Then you and I need have no further discussion. Thank you for the tea." Hermione strode toward the screen door. She was about to close the door behind her when Miranda asked a question.

"I'm curious, Mrs. Montgomery-Krausse. Did you marry Shepard's father for money? Or for love."

Hermione looked, at first, as if she would not answer. Finally, she said, "I already had money." Then she walked toward the car where her chauffeur waited. She never looked back. When she was seated in the rear seat and the car was in motion, she addressed the driver. "Did you get it?"

"Yes, madam," he answered. "And I saw no other weapons in the house."

12 THE LETTER

At dawn, Miranda sat in her front porch rocker and sipped her coffee as usual. She ignored the daily crossword puzzle. The other Magnolia Street ladies chatted together, but Miranda did not join in.

She stared at nothing, preoccupied with the confusing images in her mind: Shep and Pietro strolling arm-in-arm; Shep teasing her as she hid under a plant; Annabelle bleating about homosexuals; Shep lifting Miranda off the ground for a kiss.

Shep carrying a pink-flowered purse.

Shep landing a second kiss.

Shep's mother referring to his "disability," but not to his sexual orientation.

A third kiss.

A muscular, shirtless man jogging away from her front gate.

Miranda shook her head to sling her thoughts in a new direction. Why was she fixated on this man who was obviously unavailable, unsuitable, unfathomable, and, well, late. Where was he? He should be turning the corner by now. She stood and began walking to the front gate for a better view of the road.

"Thar she blows!" shouted Martha, looking through her binoculars. The Magnolia Street ladies leaned forward and focused on the object of their mutual obsession. Shep and Dave jogged toward them.

A change had occurred in the jogging procedure since the Day of the Snake, as it was called in Magnolia Street annals. Since that day, Shep and Dave ran along the right-hand road shoulder, no longer the left. It was a trade-off: chance another left-side rattler or give up the safety of facing oncoming traffic. Yet a third consideration clinched the left-right decision: Miranda's front gate was on the right-hand side of the road.

In fact, Miranda's house was the first house on Magnolia Street, for Shep and Dave. The other Magnolia Street ladies had come to expect that the muscle man and wonder dog would pause to exchange greetings with Miranda before resuming their run with shouts of greeting for each subsequent front porch they would pass.

The Magnolia Street ladies might have been surprised, amazed, delighted, or jealous if they had known how different Miranda's daily salutation was from their own.

"Good morning, Miz Martha! Good morning, Miz Bernice! Good morning, Miz Wyneen! Good morning, Miz Charlotte!" Shep always boomed, and waved toward each lady in turn.

Those venerable ladies did not hear the soft words Shep spoke to Miranda every morning, because Miranda left her porch and waited for the duo at her front gate.

The first time he said it, the morning after the Day of the Snake, Miranda was stunned to silence. Every day thereafter he said it.

"Good morning, Bean. Will you marry me?"

And every day, Miranda would answer, "Good morning, Mr. Krausse. No, but thank you for asking." Then she would add, "Good morning, Dave."

Dave would "whuff" and lick her fingers where they rested atop her low iron gate.

. . . .

One morning, Miranda put aside her confusion, anxiety, misgivings, and daydreams, and waited faithfully at the gate while dawn eased upward from the unseen horizon to the moss-hung treetops.

Shep and Dave stopped at her gate.

She had come to realize Dave stopped them there. Shep might have guessed approximately where she stood, but he navigated by sound and scent. Dave could see exactly where she was. Dave's cues were so subtle, and Shepard's response so automatic, it was no wonder she at first had not discerned that Shep was blind.

Shep's fingers ran lightly across the curled iron of the gate, found Miranda's hand resting there, and took it in his own. He smiled. She could see in his reflective sunglasses that she was smiling, too.

"Good morning, Bean," he said.

"Good morning, Mr. Krausse."

"'Mister Krausse' was my late father. Could you not call me Shepard, or even Shep?"

"I could call you Shepard, if that is your wish," she answered, with Librarian Formality.

"It is my dearest wish," he replied. "And by the way, will you marry me?"

"No ... Shepard ... but thank you very much for asking. May I ask you something?"

"Bean, you can ask me anything your beautiful heart desires."

She spun the question a dozen ways in her mind, trying to make it less awkward than it was doomed to be. To his credit, he waited with serene patience, stroking her hand with his thumb all the while.

Miranda took the plunge, spewing the words in a rush: "Are you—? Do you—? ... Annabelle-said-you're-gay."

She waited.

He waited.

Dave looked from one to the other. Dave waited.

Shep finally asked, "Is that a question?"

Miranda sighed. "Uh-huh."

He thought. Then he asked, "What exactly is the question?"

"Should I believe Annabelle?"

"Almost never, I think."

"About you. Or, about you and your ... friend who comes with you to the library. Should I believe Annabelle about ... that?"

"Ah, Pietro," he said. "As to 'that,' it only matters that Annabelle believes it and that she, therefore, has given up the chase where Pietro and I are concerned."

"I knew it!" Miranda exulted. "But, you know she tells everyone. She could ruin your reputation."

"My brave little Castor Bean," he crooned, "with you as my defending champion, I fear neither the Annabelle dragon nor lurking serpents nor any other evil foe."

"Whuff!" said Dave.

"We gotta go," Shep said as if taking a cue from the dog—which, of course, he was. "Sure you won't marry me?"

"Not today. Thanks."

"Be seeing ya, then," he said.

Before they resumed their run, Dave licked Miranda's fingers as always. And then Shepard pressed a warm, three-second kiss on her lips. It was the first time he had kissed her since Snake Day. He kissed even better than she remembered.

Minutes later, when Miranda had returned to her kitchen to refill her coffee cup, she realized that she had never told him of his mother's visit.

It was Saturday, and Miranda had planned to use her free day to clean out at least one of Aunt Phyllis' closets. She replayed that morning's surprise kiss in her mind while washing the breakfast dishes. Then she dug out the trash bags, tied a scarf over her hair (spider precaution), and pulled out the first cardboard file box inside the hall closet door.

The box was labeled "Audubon Society." Documents crammed into the box testified that Phyllis Ogilvy had been active in the birding group for many, many years.

Miranda sifted quickly through the papers so as not to discard any documents that should be retained for legal reasons. Her neighbor, Martha Cleary, was an Audubon member. Miranda could give Martha any papers that should be preserved by the organization in its own files.

For half the morning, papers migrated from the box to one of three piles: "trash," "keep," and "give to Martha." Really, there were only two piles. Nothing ended up in the "keep" spot. Annual bird counts and monthly newsletter archives went to Martha. Phyllis' notes to herself went to trash. Likewise the dozens of newspaper clippings covering three decades.

Miranda was stuffing the discardables into garbage bags when a handful of papers escaped and scattered across the floor. As she crawled over the papers, a familiar name leapt out at her. She picked up the document. Thin, translucent onionskin paper. Black letters in old-fashioned pica type. A manual typewriter. A date only a few weeks ago. A personal letter from Aunt Phyllis. To "Hermione Montgomery Krausse."

"She must've been ticked," murmured Miranda to herself. "Phyllis left out the hyphen."

Miranda began reading the letter. Within five seconds the Audubon Society files were forgotten. Miranda slipped into her by-the-door flip-flops, took the letter, and went out the back door. For the first time since moving in, Miranda was going to breach the dividing hedge and knock on the Krausse kitchen door.

Shepard turned off the shower and stepped out onto the plush bathroom rug. Dave stayed in the shower stall and enthusiastically shook himself dry. Shepard flicked a fluffy thick bath sheet from a wall hook. Pounding sounded in the distance. Dave stood and whined. Shepard waited, towel poised.

More pounding. The sound of the door opening. A soprano calling, "Shepard? Dave?"

"Whoopf!" said Dave and bounded happily toward the voice.

Miranda was standing in the half-open kitchen door when she was suddenly surrounded by excited, wet, gigantic dog.

"Hey, Dave," she said, and giggled as she tried to pet the rapidly circling canine.

"Bean?" said Shepard from the hallway.

Miranda looked up just as he stepped into the kitchen wearing only a towel. "Oh, my stars and garters!" Miranda cried. She spun 180 degrees and covered her eyes with one hand. "Oh, gee whiz gosh golly holy moley!"

"Hey, lady, watch your language! Dave's only seven!"

"I'm so sorry! I didn't—I just barged in—the door was unlocked and I never thought—I'm so sorry!" She was trying to be polite, but in truth she did not regret seeing the blond giant *au naturel*, or nearly so. That sublime golden image was permanently burned into her retinas. Without his sunglasses, his eyes were the ancient blue of glacier ice – which paradoxically warmed her down to her toes.

"Is there an emergency? What's happening?" asked Shepard.

"Whuff?" asked Dave.

"No. No, no emergency. I wanted to show you something," she said, still facing away from him.

He laughed. "Okay, but in the interest of not showing *you* something, I'm gonna go put some clothes on. You just have a seat, make yourself at home, visit with Dave. Won't be a minute. Okay?"

Miranda nodded. Then, when Shep didn't respond, she remembered. "Okay," she said. She heard him move off down the hallway. The bedroom door snicked closed.

She shut the half-open kitchen door and turned to face the room. Dave sat directly in front of her, watching her and —yeah, he was definitely—smiling.

"Oh, get your mind out of the gutter," she said.

"Whuff," said Dave.

. . . .

Ten minutes later Miranda and Shepard were sitting at the kitchen table. Shepard wore close-fitting old jeans and a tee shirt that accentuated his broad shoulders, six-pack abs, and melon-size biceps. He was still toweling his hair.

When Miranda could force herself beyond simply appreciating the view from across the table, she explained that she had found something strange among Phyllis' personal papers. "But before I tell you what I found, I need to tell you something else."

"Fire away," Shepard said, draping the towel about his neck. He began combing the tangles from his hair. Miranda was mesmerized by the white-gold mane that ended between his shoulder blades. Her eyes followed the comb as it stroked again and again through the silky strands. "Bean?"

"Oh! Sorry. Distracted." She gave her head a clearing shake. "Your mother came to see me a few days ago."

He froze. "My m—? Are you sure it was *my* mother?"

"Pretty sure."

"Tall lady? Nose in the air? Queen-of-England gloves? Chauffeur?"

"Exactly."

He put down his comb and gathered the hair into a ponytail, which he secured with an elastic band he'd worn on his wrist. "Well, dog my cats," he murmured. "Were you scared?"

"What?" She was genuinely surprised.

"Hermione can be pretty scary," Shep commented.

"Whuff," agreed Dave.

Miranda smiled at their concern. "I was impressed, that's for sure! But I wasn't afraid. It was nice to get to know her."

"*Nice?*"

"Okay, maybe not really 'nice,' but it was ... interesting," Miranda said. "See, at the time, I was thinking you and Pietro were a, uh, couple, y'know?"

"Annabelle's gay theory."

"Right. So, I was confused when your mother sort of told me not to, uh, set my cap for you."

Shep grinned. "Your cap?"

"She was telling me not to plan on marrying you. That I'm not, uh, the right type I guess?"

"And you were wondering why my own mother apparently didn't know I was gay." Shep was smiling.

"I thought maybe you were, uh, in the closet where your parents are concerned."

"But now you know better," he said.

"Yes. Now I know," she agreed.

"And what did you say?"

"What did I say? About what?"

"About marrying me. What did you say?" Shepard asked.

"Oh. That." Miranda hesitated. "I think I said something like 'I've not yet encountered the man I plan to marry,' or words to that effect."

Shepard shook his head in mock distress. "Beeeeean! Bean-Bean-Bean-Bean-Beeeean! What have you done?"

"Pardon?"

He parodied disappointment in the extreme. "You lied to my sainted mother!"

"I did nothing of the kind!" Miranda was insulted. "How dare you impugn my integrity!?"

In his most soothing tones, he explained: "You most certainly have encountered your future marital partner, Castor Bean. He is me."

"Stop your teasing!" She punched his huge arm and laughed. "He is not you, or you are not he. Whatever. In fact, Dave and I may elope the moment your back is turned."

"Whuff!" agreed Dave.

"*Et tu*, Dave?" Shepard intoned.

"Can I tell you what I came for now?" asked Miranda. She shook the onionskin document brought from Phyllis' Audubon carton. Shepard reacted to the crackle of the paper.

"What is it?"

"It's a letter Aunt Phyllis wrote ... to your mother!"

"And that's strange because...?"

"Your mother acted like she had never been in that house before. Like she never knew my aunt."

Shepard thought. His index finger tapped the tabletop four times before he answered, "I doubt my mother has ever been inside Phyllis' house, come to think of it. They were not what I would describe as 'close.' But they definitely knew each other. Since they were kids, I expect.

"After all, Phyllis was the girl-next-door to my father during his entire childhood. Hermione went to an expensive private school—the Montgomerys always did—but Phyllis and my dad went to public school together all the way through high school."

Miranda took a moment to assimilate the information. "Then, it's more strange than I thought!"

"Why? They were acquainted their whole lives. Nothing strange about a friend writing a letter to another friend," Shepard said.

"But the letter reads like they hadn't been speaking to each other for a very long time, Shep. Phyllis even apologizes for breaking their silence. Like she wasn't supposed to contact your parents ... ever. And vice versa. Is that how it was between them?" Miranda asked.

Shep was quiet. Remembering. He nodded and said, "It could've been that way. My dad brought me to see my grandparents often, and I always spent time with Phyllis. But my mother almost never came to Minokee. And after they were married, neither of my parents ever went over to Phyllis' house.

"I was a child. I was happy visiting my friend Phyllis. I guess I wasn't conscious of bad blood between Phyllis and my parents. My grandparents loved her."

The kitchen clock clicked off ten, fifteen, twenty, thirty seconds while Miranda and Shepard sorted through their separate thoughts. Finally, Shep rose from the table. "How about a glass of sweet tea? Then you can read me that letter."

Minutes later, over iced sweet tea, Miranda read to Shep and Dave the carbon copy of Phyllis Ogilvy's recent letter to Hermione Montgomery-without-the-darn-hyphen-Krausse. It was dated six weeks earlier — or two weeks before Phyllis Ogilvy died.

"Dear Hermie," it began.

"If you have opened this envelope rather than tossing it out, I am already obliged to you. Please forgive me for violating our pledge of silence. I assure you I do not break my vow without good cause. Not for my sake, but for the sake of those whom both you and I have loved, please continue reading until the end.

"Although I will mark the envelope 'personal and confidential,' the reality is that your personal assistant or corresponding secretary may, in fact, open and read such letters for you as a matter of course. For that reason, I will identify all parties by childhood names only you and I will remember. The need for such secrecy will shortly become obvious.

"Quite by accident, while conducting an Audubon Society field survey of Wood Stork nesting sites, I photographed two rats. Or perhaps weasels. I had hiked deep into the Little Cypress National Forest that surrounds Minokee. There at the end of an old logging road were two parked cars. Iggy was the driver of one. The other man you would readily recognize from numerous newspaper photos published of late.

"The man has been widely suspected of criminal activity. The key word to describe it would be the same as your least favorite part of a game of bridge.

"Iggy has stated publicly and often that he does not know this man and has never had business dealings with him. I regret to say that I have several very clear photographs showing an exchange of envelopes between the two men. If their relationship were to become known, both men could end up in prison.

"The one person in the whole world to whom Iggy might listen, Hermie, is you. Can you not persuade Iggy to step forward, denounce the scandalous actions of this man, make restitution to those whose businesses have been harmed by those actions, and publicly apologize? How much better for Iggy to be the heroic figure who stands for justice and truth — rather than to deny his crimes until confronted with damning and incontrovertible evidence!

"I know that Iggy could lose his present job, and he almost certainly would not receive the big promotion everyone expects for him in the near future. But he could receive a shorter prison term, gain public sympathy, and take pride in having done the right thing. He will never be able to hold his head up again if these pictures are made public.

"You may say Iggy is an adult and should reap what he has sown. And this is true. But stop a moment and consider someone else whose future could be ruined. Think about Speedy. True, he has not yet begun to pursue the future I know you wish for him. But that future awaits him. It needs only for him to decide the time is right, and he will begin a meteoric rise to levels of power and success about which one can only dream.

"I wish I did not have this horrible responsibility. But the evidence fell to me, and I am committed to doing the right thing. I will wait until the first of the month — that is three weeks from now. If by that time Iggy has not come forward on his own, I will deliver the evidence to the State Attorney. I would not stand by and see Speedy's life destroyed, nor, I think, can you.

"I do not wish to sully anyone's good name. I do not wish to see Iggy arrested and tried like a common gangster. You are my last, best hope of resolving the situation as positively as possible.

"Thank you for perusing what has been hard to write and must be incredibly difficult to read. I will say nothing of this to anyone else. I resume our pledge of silence. You will never hear from me again.

"Sincerely,

"Phil."

Miranda folded the letter and waited for Shepard's reaction.

"Wow," he breathed.

"Yeah, wow," said Miranda. "She said she would go public in three weeks. But two weeks later, she died."

"Yeah."

"Do you know what she was talking about? Who these people are?"

"I don't know anybody called 'Iggy,' but I do know Speedy," Shepard said. "Phyllis used to compare me to the cartoon boy in an old television commercial—big eyes, big smile, lots of yellow hair. She called me 'Speedy Alka-Seltzer' for years."

Miranda was silent, turning the letter over and over in her hands. Shepard absently stroked Dave's head and neck.

"Do you think Iggy is a gangster?" Miranda asked, barely audibly.

"Dunno," Shep said.

"Shepard..." Miranda couldn't force the question from her throat.

"You wanna know if I think Hermione told Iggy about Phyllis and the pictures."

"Not just that," Miranda said. "If this Iggy guy really is a gangster, ... well, ... do you think he had Aunt Phyllis killed?"

"I don't know. But the timing would be about right, wouldn't it."

"But she had a heart attack, right?" Miranda whispered.

"Do you want to have the body exhumed for an autopsy? Maybe it wasn't a heart attack. Lots of things can be made to look like a heart attack – especially if the authorities have been...influenced...to see it that way."

Miranda shook her head. She was thinking he had not put on his sunglasses after his shower.

"Miranda?" said Shepard softly, finding her hand on the table and covering it with his own.

"What?"

"Autopsy?"

"Oh!" Miranda shook off her wayward thoughts. "No, sorry. Aunt Phyllis was cremated. That's why we had a 'memorial service' rather than a 'funeral.'" She used her fingers to form quotation marks in the air, then made a wry face and flapped her hands before dropping them to her lap. Trite gestures – any gestures – were wasted on those blue eyes.

Shepard stood purposefully. Dave jumped to his feet and moved immediately to his master's side, ready to go.

"What are you going to do?" asked Miranda.

"First," he said, "I'm going to call my mother."

Miranda excused herself to return to her closet-cleaning chore — and to give Shepard privacy in which to talk to his mother. As she let herself out the Krausse kitchen door, Shep was punching Hermione's number into the phone.

13 THE TEA

Hermione had been more than a little surprised to receive a call from her only son on a Saturday morning. Usually if she wanted to hear his voice she had to listen to his abominable radio program in the wee hours. Occasionally, she would have her personal assistant place a call to Shepard. Nine times out of ten, Hermione would be too busy to pick up the phone immediately, however, and Shep would usually hang up after holding for two or three minutes.

It was frustrating to actually have Shepard on the phone yet not have a real conversation with him. He only wanted to set up a visit—perhaps tea on Sunday afternoon.

"Marvelous!" Hermione told him. "Three-thirty. I'll have Cook bake those tortes you like."

"Set an extra place for Bean," Shep said. "She'll be driving."

"Bean?" Hermione's voice was cold. "You're bringing someone named after produce?"

"It's a nickname. You've met her, actually. Phyllis Ogilvy's niece." Shep waited a long time while his mother processed the unwelcome news and constructed what, to her, would be a tactful response.

"Indeed," was Hermione's careful reply. "I understood that she was not ... involved ... with anyone. Are you telling me she is involved with *you*?"

Shep laughed. "She's involved. She just doesn't know it yet. See you tomorrow, Mother."

They disconnected. Hermione didn't pretend she was looking forward to it.

Miranda agonized about what to wear to tea with the queen mum, but in the end it made little difference. Every outfit Miranda owned fell into one of two categories: Librarian/Nun or Servant/Urchin. She wore the first style.

She was ready when Shep and Dave knocked on her back door. She grabbed her purse and keys and led them around the side of the house to her tiny, second-hand commuter car. Dave led Shep to the passenger side of the car, and Miranda opened the door. Shep ran his hands over the door, the miniature seat, and the roof—which didn't reach as high as his armpits.

"Is this your car?" he asked Miranda. When she said yes, he continued, "Where's the rest of it? There's not, like, a side car or a trailer or something?"

She said no.

"Maybe Dave should stay home," Shep said.

"Nonsense. There's plenty of room—well, not plenty of room, but—there's room for Dave in the back. He won't mind. Will you, Dave?"

Dave whined.

Miranda bent down to look in his eyes and pat his head. "You'll be fine. I've ridden back there."

"It's small enough, you can probably *drive* from back there!" quipped Shepard.

Miranda turned on Shepard. "You're not helping."

He shrugged.

She turned back to Dave. "C'mon. Try something new. Don't be a big baby like you-know-who." She poked a thumb over her shoulder toward Shepard.

"I saw that," he said.

"No, you didn't," she said. She raised her eyebrows at Dave and gestured with one arm toward the open car door.

"Whuff," said Dave, and wormed his way into the miniscule back seat. From outside the car, the rear window appeared to be a shag carpet.

Miranda turned to Shepard. "Your turn."

He began angling to squeeze into the passenger seat. "I'm pretty sure I've got a duffle bag that's bigger than this," he said. "I've never tried to sit in it, though. Maybe when we get back I'll do that. Just for comparison."

"Yeah, yeah, yeah, you're both a couple of whiners," said Miranda. "Man up!" She closed the passenger door and circled the hood to climb into the driver's seat.

Miranda drove for over an hour with Dave's lolling tongue hanging beside her left ear. Shepard's shoulders touched the passenger window on the right and the driver's seat on the left. Miranda knew she would later find long, golden hairs snagged in the overhead fabric where his head had rubbed the ceiling.

. . . .

Miranda's overloaded mini-car chugged through electrically opened security gates and onto a vast circular driveway. Miranda thought that if two driveways like this one were placed as mirror images, they would comprise an oval the size of the Daytona Speedway.

She parked at the apex of the driveway arc, directly in front of massive double doors opening off a snowy-marble colonnade that spanned the mansion's facade. The house seemed a football field wide. It was three stories plus gables projecting from the attic level. That meant to Miranda that small rooms for the servants made up the fourth floor.

Shepard unfolded himself from the car with exaggerated moans and elaborate stretching. Dave squirmed out the driver's side door because there was no room for him to turn around and exit on the passenger side. Dave went immediately to Shepard's side, where Dave executed his own yawning and stretching.

"Very funny," Miranda said.

Shepard was all innocence. "What?"

As they walked up the wide steps toward the front door, Miranda said, "You're better than a GPS system. I've never received such specific, accurate directions from anyone before. 'Take County Road 162 west for three-tenths of a mile, then turn right on Weaver's Mill Road and go north for two point three miles....' Who gives directions like that?"

Shepard chuckled. "What, did you think I'd use landmarks? 'Turn right at the yellow house with the blue birdbath?'"

"Point taken," said Miranda.

Dave stopped at the front door, and Shepard rang the doorbell. Miranda looked surprised.

"It's your mom's house. You don't just walk in?"

"Not unless I develop a death wish."

The huge doors divided ponderously, revealing a black-clad butler. He did not smile, but stepped aside and gestured for them to enter. "Good afternoon, Mr. Shepard. Madam is expecting you. Please go through to the east parlor."

"Good afternoon, Hanson. This is my neighbor, Miss Ogilvy. She was ... is ... *was* Miss Phyllis' niece," said Shepard.

"Nice to meet you, Mr. Hanson," Miranda said, extending her hand.

"Just 'Hanson,' miss," said the butler. He did not shake her hand. "Sorry for your loss." He didn't sound particularly sorrowful.

"Thank you, ... Hanson," Miranda said, retracting her hand awkwardly.

Shepard placed a hand on Dave's back and said, "East parlor, Dave." Dave led the way, with Shep and Miranda following. "Safer to let Dave navigate," Shep whispered. "Mother's always rearranging the furnishings."

They arrived at the parlor entrance like characters out of *The Wizard of Oz*: a dowdy Good Witch accompanied by an impaired Viking and a lion-size bandana-wearing beast. If flying monkeys had suddenly launched themselves from the room's eight-foot ficus trees, Miranda would have taken it in stride.

Seeing the odd trio in the doorway, Hermione rose from her seat at the tea table. Her silk cocktail pajamas billowed gracefully as she glided across the room and gave Shepard a

Euro-kiss on each cheek. "So glad to have you, dear," she said. "Please be seated."

Hermione neither looked at nor spoke to Miranda. Dave and Miranda were nudged aside as Hermione stepped to Shepard's side and put her hand on his elbow as if to guide him.

"I've got this, Mother," said Shepard, withdrawing his elbow and reaching around her to touch Dave.

Hermione returned to her chair. Shepard followed Dave to the table, where Shep pulled back a chair and seated Miranda before sitting down beside her. Dave lay down beside Shepard's chair.

"It's nice to see you again, Mrs. Montgomery-Krausse," said Miranda.

Hermione did not raise her eyes above the exquisite silver teapot from which she was pouring. "I hadn't expected to meet you again, Miss Ogilvy. So soon, I mean." She passed a delicate tea-filled cup to Miranda and then one to Shepard. "Will you have milk, sugar, or lemon, Shepard?"

Miranda noticed his mother looked up when speaking to Shepard. When Shepard declined condiments for his tea, Hermione made no such offer to Miranda. Miranda smiled and helped herself to milk and sugar.

Hermione lifted a crystal plate of tea sandwiches and pastries and set it beside Shepard's saucer. "Cucumber sandwiches and Black Forest torte," she said proudly, "as promised."

"Wonderful," Shepard said, and offered the plate to Miranda before selecting anything for himself.

"Shepard, dear, you are always welcome, you know that."

"Thank you, Mother."

"Yes. Well, ever since you telephoned yesterday I have been wondering about the occasion for this unexpected visit. You, ah, you're not announcing an engagement or anything, are you?"

"No!" Miranda said.

"Not yet," Shepard said.

"It isn't 'not yet,' Shepard, it's no. N. O." Miranda clarified.

"I see," said Hermione in a tone that belied the words. "What is it, then? Are you changing jobs? Moving from the woods back into the city? Preparing to run for office at long last?"

Shepard took a moment to chew and swallow a circular, bite-size sandwich. "Who is Iggy?" he said, too casually.

A lesser matriarch might have choked on her torte or sloshed the tea from her Limoges cup, but Hermione Montgomery hyphen Krausse was made of sterner stuff. She reacted not at all. Just as casually, she answered, "I don't believe I know anyone named—Eggy, was it?"

"Iggy."

"Iggy. Nnn-no, I don't recall meeting an Iggy. Who is he? Or she, as the case may be?"

Shepard shrugged. "Dunno. Phyllis mentioned him."

"Not recently, I trust," Hermione said with a bitter smile.

"Why have you and my aunt been estranged for the last thirty years?" Miranda spurted. For the first time that afternoon, Hermione looked Miranda directly in the eyes. It was not a friendly look.

"If you must know, Miss Ogilvy, your aunt was in love with my husband. More fool she, because he chose me. We all knew how Phyllis felt. We thought it best to sever all contact and avoid any unpleasantness or misunderstanding.

"The fact that Phyllis never married, I believe, proves that we made a wise decision. Neither she nor my husband were forced to contend with awkward social situations or temptation of a salacious nature."

"Salacious?" asked Miranda. "Aunt Phyllis?"

Hermione's voice was hard and strong: "Garrett Krausse was the love of her life. I did them both a favor by making it a clean break."

Miranda reeled mentally and sat back in her chair to sort the ideas piling into her head.

Shepard let the silence breathe for a moment before he asked quietly, "Did Phyllis ever contact you—after Dad died, maybe?"

"Why should she?" Hermione was abrupt. "Garrett was dead. Phyllis and I had nothing in common any more."

"Nothing in common?" he asked. "Not even me? Not even Iggy?"

His mother ignored all but the last. "I told you, I don't know anyone called Iggy."

Shepard finished his last sip of tea, folded his linen napkin carefully, placed it beside his saucer, and stood. Dave scrambled up immediately.

"What are you doing?" asked Hermione.

Shepard pulled back Miranda's chair and offered her a hand to rise. "Thank you for an enlightening visit, Mother, but we really need to be getting back to the woods. I find the air in the city especially oppressive this afternoon."

"Thank you for tea, Mrs. Montgomery-Krausse," murmured Miranda. She followed as Dave led Shepard toward the exit.

Hermione jumped to her feet with considerably less aplomb than when they'd first arrived. "But you can't go! It's too soon! You've only just arrived!"

Shepard stopped and turned to face her. "Too soon? For what?"

His mother stammered uncharacteristically, "Um, well, i-i-it's too soon to get back into a stuffy automobile. You've scarcely had time to cool down from your long drive."

"Cool down, Mother?" Shepard spoke as if exercising great self-control. "I'm afraid if I stay much longer I won't be cool at all, I'll be 'hot under the collar,' as the saying goes. Then this visit could deteriorate into one of those 'awkward social situations' you've spent thirty years avoiding. Allow me to wish you good day. Perhaps we'll speak again when I have indeed 'cooled down.'"

Hermione was silent and still while her visitors left the house.

In the car a half-hour later, Shepard broke the silence for the first time since leaving his mother's mansion.

"Well," he said, "Phyllis is dead, Hermione is lying, and I still have two questions. Who, who, who might have the answers?"

"Depends," said Miranda. "What are the two questions?"

"Who is Iggy? And where did Phyllis put the pictures?"

"Mmm," said Miranda. Dave panted into her left ear while she thought.

Shepard shifted in his seat, trying to keep the vibrating passenger window from bruising his shoulder. The little car chugged valiantly, maxed out at a racy fifty miles per hour.

"Oh, and I have one other question," said Shepard.

"What?"

"Bean, will you marry me?"

"Not today. But thanks for asking."

"You're very welcome," he said. They finished the trip in comfortable silence.

14 THE TROPHY

Monday morning, Miranda the Invisible Librarian was re-shelving books in the self-improvement section, enjoying the quiet and the smell of the Starbucks lattes smuggled in by the college students working in the nearby reference section. She had just placed a well-worn copy of *Thirty Theorems on Thicker Hair and Thinner Thighs* when Annabelle poked her head around the corner.

"Miriam, there's a delivery for you at the front desk."

Miranda started to say, "Be right th—," but realized she was talking to air.

At the desk, a forty-ish balding gnome with wire-rimmed glasses and a handlebar mustache waited with a package wrapped in white butcher paper. It looked like a seven-foot submarine sandwich. The gnome didn't see Miranda approach, though he was facing in her direction.

Accustomed to the phenomenon, Miranda stopped in front of the oblivious little man and spoke softly, "May I help you?"

He jumped and nearly dropped his package. His eyes jerked to Miranda's face and focused. "H-how did you do that?" He glanced left and right beyond her as if he would discover where she had been hiding.

Miranda's smile was resigned. "It's a gift. Is that for me?" She gestured at the parcel.

"You Marguerite Ogilvy?"

"I'm Miranda Ogilvy."

He looked at the label on the package. "Close enough. Gotcher rattler." He pushed the parcel toward her, but she didn't reach to take it.

"I'm sorry. Did you say something about rats?" Wild horses couldn't get her to touch that package. Seven feet of rats?

"Rattler," he said, loudly and slowly. "I said 'I got yer rattler' for ya." He smiled proudly. "Mounted it myself. She's a beauty, too. Congratulations."

Annabelle, stunning in a low-cut, tight-waisted, short-skirted red dress, leaned way across the counter toward the man. "What did you say you mounted, sugar?" she purred.

The man's mouth dropped open and his eyes bulged when he turned to see Annabelle and her girls mere inches from his right shoulder. He forgot Marguerite Ogilvy ever existed and rotated to face Annabelle. "Huh?" he breathed.

Annabelle smiled—half Marilyn Monroe, half cobra—and walked her fingers up his shirtfront. "Were you talkin' about mountin' somethin'," she looked at the name on his shirt, "Ray?"

Ray snapped out of it, overcome with pride in his accomplishment. "Oh, yes, ma'am! I mounted this here snakeskin for Miz Oglethorpe. Six footer, mint condition—except for the missin' head—and a lovely mahogany platform. Look here!"

Before she could stop him, the man had begun tearing paper away and shoving the mahogany plank onto the counter, forcing Annabelle to stand up and back away. Miranda stepped in to look over Ray's shoulder. Within seconds they were looking down at Miranda's trophy rattlesnake skin, professionally affixed to shining rich dark wood.

"Lovely," said Annabelle, meaning, of course, the opposite.

"Is this the snake I shot?" asked Miranda.

"Are you Marianne Oglethorpe?" asked Ray, surprised to find someone standing beside him.

"Close enough," said Miranda. "But who did this?" She spread her arms to indicate the massive trophy.

Ray produced a folded invoice from his pocket and shook it open. "Order was placed by Mrs. Martha Cleary out in Minokee. She brung us the corpse, and I took care of it personally."

Miranda read the figure at the bottom of the invoice. She gasped. "But Martha can't afford this! Neither can I, for that matter!"

"Oh, don't sweat the money," Ray said, folding and pocketing the invoice. "I already got a check from the Shep and Dave Show. Why some crackpot radio program would be buying somebody a snake is a mystery to me, but that's life, ain't it? Ya think you've seen it all, but...." He shrugged.

He admired his product in silence. Miranda looked from one end of the reptile to the other and back again. Annabelle got bored and walked away.

"What am going to do with it?" asked Miranda of herself, but Ray heard and answered.

"Hang it on the wall! Be proud! Tell the story to your friends! Thing like this is priceless!" He patted it fondly as if saying farewell to a pet. "Y'know what's weird?"

Miranda's eyes widened. "There's more!?"

"I don't wanna go into too much detail, but part of the job was to separate the outside of the snake from the inside of the snake. Know what I mean?"

When she nodded uncertainly, Ray continued. "Y'see, this feller had eaten not long afore he 'uz kilt. And he hadn't been livin' in the wild. No, ma'am, he 'uz chowing down on domestic white mice—like lab mice, y'know. He didn't get those in the Little Cypress."

"That doesn't make any sense," Miranda said. "Where would a wild snake get white laboratory rodents to eat?"

"Weren't no wild snake," Ray said. "This snake 'uz somebody's pet." He looked at Miranda in mock accusation. "You sure you don't have a neighbor mad atcha fer shootin' Fluffy here?" He laughed at his own joke and moved toward the door. "Congratulations again!" he called as he left.

Miranda stared down at the bizarre memento spread across the library counter.

Annabelle's voice wafted to her from the office beyond a partition, "For pity's sake, Myrtle, take that awful thing and put it out in your car before somebody comes in and sees it!"

My car! thought Miranda, and spread her arms to measure the length of her trophy. *Maybe if I hang it out the window?*

15 THE GOVERNOR

On the same Monday that Miranda received her snake from Ray the taxidermist, a snake of another kind rode in his limousine through the electric gates of the Montgomery-Krausse estate. There was no great fanfare. Security was casual, the entourage limited to a handful of discreet, trusted minions. No big deal. Just the governor having lunch with his sister.

The black-suited butler opened the massive double doors before the governor reached the top veranda step. Reginald Jackson Montgomery could not be kept waiting at the door, in fact could not be expected to break his stride as he traversed from limo to dining room.

Hermione greeted Reginald at the door of the cavernous formal dining room. They exchanged their customary cheek-pecks. Reginald ushered his elegantly dressed sister to her chair, then seated himself at her right—at the head of the twenty-person table. The unseen butler softly closed the dining room doors.

Miranda would have thought the scene ludicrous, but to the pampered pair of diners it seemed mundane. The room held two priceless Tiffany chandeliers, eighteen empty upholstered chairs, a 500-year-old Turkish carpet, and a fresh flower centerpiece the size of a small refrigerator. China, crystal, and sterling silver, together with linen napkins, awaited only two people. Presumably their gourmet repast would pass through guts and gullets no different from those of any commoner, however.

Ignoring their surroundings and all their obvious reasons to be grateful, the siblings began eating without a word of grace. Praying was something Reginald did only in public and Hermione did not at all. They were their own gods. But all was not sunny atop Olympus this day.

"Well, I'm here," the governor growled between bites of salmon mousse. "What was so important that I had to reschedule three meetings to get here?"

Hermione took her time swallowing her latest mouthful, placing her silver utensil carefully on her gold-rimmed plate, dabbing her lips with her linen.

"I recall telling you that Phyllis Ogilvy would come back and bite you in the ass someday, Reggie," said Hermione. "I'm afraid that day may be upon us."

"Nonsense," Reginald said. "Phyllis is dead."

"But my son is not dead, and he apparently has read Phyllis' letter. He was here asking questions about it yesterday afternoon. And Phyllis' frumpy niece was with him."

"That letter was destroyed. All Shepard has is the rumors he spreads on his idiotic talk show." Reginald continued eating, unperturbed.

Hermione put her hand on his forearm and stopped his fork in mid-air. "I destroyed the original letter, yes, but this is Phyllis we're talking about. She always was compulsive about books and papers. Her house is probably like an archive—file cabinets or boxes of files in every closet. She probably kept carbon copies of every grocery list she ever made, much less what she would consider 'official correspondence'!"

Reginald shook her hand away lightly and continued eating. "You know the nice thing about paper, Hermie?"

"What?"

"It burns," said Reginald.

"What are you saying? That you would commit arson? Add another crime to your *curriculum vitae*? You'll ruin us all! Aren't there enough skeletons already waiting to spring from the closet at the worst possible moment?"

"Keep your voice down," he said. "No crime. I'm not stupid. But anyone will tell you those old shacks in Minokee are nothing but firetraps, what with all that dried out wood and frayed, inadequate wiring."

"And the niece who lives there?" asked Hermione, not concerned, but curious.

"Perhaps she won't be at home," Reginald said.

Hermione picked up her fork and prepared to finish her lunch. "I don't care what happens to the little busybody, but hear me well, Reggie. Nothing and no one is to raise a hand against Shepard. If anything happens to my son because of something you've said or done, you'll be very sorry."

"I imagine you'd withdraw your considerable financial support," he acknowledged. "I would expect no less, and you would be justified in doing so. Don't worry. My nephew is a fly in my ointment, but he is no danger to me, Hermie dear."

"Good," she said. "Because—and let me make myself absolutely clear—you harm Shepard in any way, and I will obliterate you, Reggie dear."

She said it with all the emotion she might have invested in suggesting a good movie. And they both knew she was deadly serious. They had grown up together. Reginald was the peacock, more visible and colorful than the hen. Hermione was the mother grizzly bear with a cub to protect.

They polished off their meal. Reggie said the Black Forest torte was extremely good. Then it was kiss-kiss, butler-door, limo-gate, and life went on as usual.

16 THE ARSONIST

Pietro bustled about the Krausse kitchen making dinner. He was stirring the tomato sauce for his chicken cacciatore when Shepard and Dave entered the room. Dave smelled like expensive shower gel and moisturizing hair conditioner. Pietro got a whiff of the dog, shook his head and sighed.

"Before you sit down," Pietro told Shepard, "your message light is blinking."

"I really hope it's not my mother," Shep said, moving to the counter where the machine squatted. "I had enough personal time with mom yesterday to last me a long time."

Shep punched the playback button. The message was from Miranda. He smiled when he heard her voice. Pietro glanced at Shep, then glanced again and chuckled.

"Hi, Shepard, this is Miranda," the voice announced (unnecessarily). "I'm going to do some shopping in town after work tonight, and I may not get home before you leave for work. I wanted to thank you for the, uh, impressive gift. The taxidermist delivered it today. What a surprise. Ahm, I can't really get it in my car? Don't laugh. So maybe you can help me work out a way to bring it home—at a time that's convenient for you, of course.

"So, ahm, thank you. That's my excuse for calling. But that's not really what I called about. Shep, that snake wasn't from the wild, it had been fed by someone. It was a captive animal, or a pet. I think somebody put it in the road that morning. They had to be nearby to time it just right, then they hid and let you run right onto it. I'm not usually an alarmist, but ... Shepard, be very careful. I think someone tried to kill you.

"Well, let me go, I'm using up your whole tape or memory card or whatever. See you soon. 'Bye."

Pietro turned from his stove and opened his mouth to say something, but Shepard forestalled him with a raised finger. "Don't you dare say 'I told you so.'"

"The only thing I gonna say is ... is, uh ... "

"How about 'dinner's ready'?"

"Yeah, thatsa what I gonna say. Dinner she'sa ready. Everybody sit."

Shep sat down at the table. Dave sat attentively beside his feeding mat on the floor.

. . . .

It was dark in the deep shade of Minokee's overhanging oaks long before it was dark in wide-open parts of the county. Central Florida's rolling treeless pasturelands held a twilight until after nine, in the summer, but in Minokee on this Monday evening, it was plenty dark by eight.

On Orchid Street, Pietro and Shepard were finishing the dishes and preparing to load up for the long drive into Live Oak for their night shift. Dave was dozing on the cool tile floor of the kitchen.

On Magnolia Street, Miranda was hefting grocery bags out of her car. She entered through the kitchen door and set the bags on the counter near the refrigerator.

That's when he hit her.

Miranda crashed to the terrazzo floor. Sledgehammers of pain bashed her knees and elbows. Her face slapped the cold terrazzo; lightning flashed behind her eyelids. Her hipbone scraped across the floor as she tried to roll aside. He snatched her up by the arm, nearly dislocating her shoulder. She yelped in pain.

"Quiet!" he snarled. "Get in there!" He virtually tossed her across the kitchen. She reeled into the living room and fell half on the floor, half on the sofa.

On Orchid Street, Dave jerked to a stand and WHOOPFED in his outdoor voice.

Shep and Pietro turned to see what this unusual behavior meant. "Whatever it is, it's not good," Shep said.

Dave leaped to the kitchen door and scratched frantically, whining and barking his alarm. Pietro threw open the door and stepped back to avoid being trampled. He leaned out and watched the dog speed away.

"He'sa go through the hedge!" Pietro yelled.

"Follow him!" Shep shouted.

Pietro raced out the door in Dave's wake. Shepard followed.

. . . .

On Magnolia Street, Miranda struggled to focus her blurred vision, but the man was only a blacker shape in the darkness. Then suddenly he was silhouetted against flames. Miranda's kitchen was burning.

Abruptly a huge, wolf-like form burst through the half-open back door and leaped upon the man shape.

When Shep reached the hedge, Pietro met him, returning as fast as he'd left. "Fire!" Pietro shouted. "I'll get the extinguisher!" He sped on toward the house.

"Miranda!" cried Shepard. He ran in the direction of her house.

Something slammed into his neck; his feet flew forward without him.

He hit the ground flat on his back.

"Damned clothesline," he muttered through gritted teeth.

Shepard was working his way to a standing position, hoping nothing important was broken, when Pietro passed him, panting heavily. Shep knew Pietro had the fire extinguisher.

In the flaming kitchen, the wolf shape and the man shape plummeted to the floor and rolled. The man grappled desperately, trying to keep deadly fangs from ripping his throat. The animal was heavy and strong and highly motivated. Bloodcurdling snarls vied with the fire's roar in Miranda's ears.

Miranda dragged her aching limbs from the sofa and crawled toward the hall closet. The shotgun. If she could only reach the shotgun.

Pietro barreled into the kitchen and spewed fire-suppressing foam toward a wall of flame.

Miranda inched toward the closet. She hurt all over and could barely see. The hallway seemed no closer than when she had begun her agonizing crawl.

On the living room floor, the man shape forced a black-clad forearm into Dave's attacking jaws long enough for the man to reach into a pocket with the other arm.

Shep burst past the fiery kitchen, heard the struggle on the floor, and shouted, "Dave! Leave it! Dave! Back off!"

Dave backed off the man just as the man swiped at Dave's belly with the knife he had pulled from his pocket. Dave barked and snarled and bared his fangs at the man.

Seeing himself outnumbered by Shep, Pietro, and an extremely dangerous Dave, the man scrambled to his feet and fled out the front door. Dave, barking, almost followed.

"Dave! Stay!" commanded Shepard. "Miranda! Miranda! Are you here?! Miranda!"

"I'm here," a weak voice mewed in the darkness.

"Fire's out!" Pietro shouted from the kitchen. "Checking for hot spots now."

Shepard took a step toward Miranda's voice. "Where are you, Miranda?" he called.

"Closet," she exhaled. He found her in two seconds.

"Are you hurt?" he said, squatting on the floor where she sat propped against the open hall closet door.

"Just bruises," she whispered.

"Poor little Bean," he said, and lifted her into his arms as easily as he would a small child. He stood a moment, then called, "Dave!"

Dave came immediately to his side, whined once, and licked Miranda's ankles where they hung down from Shep's embrace.

"Couch, please, Dave," said Shepard, and Dave moved to the couch, fur brushing against Shepard's leg all the way.

Shepard gently laid Miranda on the sofa and sat beside her. "Shotgun," she murmured.

"What about it, baby?" he whispered, taking her small hand and enfolding it between both of his.

She looked at him in great puzzlement. "It's gone," she said.

Pietro flicked on a table lamp at one end of the sofa. "I thinka the wiring she is safe in this room," he said. "Only thing burned isa da kitchen cabinets near da sink."

"Thanks," said Shep.

"I'ma gonna call the law," said Pietro. "We lucky tonight. Dave, he save da day dis time, but somebody coulda been dead. You listenin' to me, Shepard Krausse?"

"After you call the county sheriff," Shep said, "go across the street and ask Martha to come—"

"Martha's done come," her unmistakable voice resonated from the open front door. "Bernice is here, too. Wyneen's done called the sheriff, and Charlotte's talking to the volunteer fire department about sending someone over to check everthing out, be sure nothin's smolderin' nowheres."

"Thanks, Martha," said Shep.

"How's our girly?" Martha asked.

Shep stood, and Martha took his seat on the couch.

Shep held Miranda's hand a moment longer before placing it gently on her stomach. "She says just bruises. Can you stay awhile? Until the sheriff comes and goes, at least?"

"Now, Shepard Krausse, you know me and Bernice ain't leavin' this chile tonight. We'll take care of her right here until the law comes, and after they go I'm takin' little missy home with me tonight. She ain't stayin' in this house alone agin 'til she's good and ready."

Bernice had come to stand at the end of the sofa. She nodded her agreement.

"He cain't see ya, Bernice," groused Martha.

"Don't worry 'bout nothin', Shep. We got this 'un," Bernice said. "I'll be back in a minute with some ice for those bruises."

"Appreciate it," Shep said as Bernice went out the front door almost as fast as the arsonist had done.

"Thank you," breathed Miranda. Gallons of adrenaline had flooded her body and were now evaporating. Her eyes just would not stay open. She had so much to say to Shepard, and she wanted to tell everyone how much she loved them and was grateful for their help. *So much to do ... huge mess ... groceries... probably ruined... picked me up ...gee, I guess those muscles aren't just for show ... is this what shock feels like?*

"Go to sleep, Castor Bean," whispered Shepard. He leaned down and kissed her forehead. He removed her glasses and handed them to Martha. "Pietro and I have to go to work. Tell the deputy we'll stop by and make a statement before we leave Live Oak in the morning."

"Right-o," said Martha. She patted him on the arm.

"Dave, home," said Shep. He put one hand on Dave's back and they left. Pietro joined them as they walked toward the hedge.

"I can'ta wait to hear what you gonna say on da air tonight. We still alive. I know you gonna keep talkin' 'til somebody make us dead. Look out for da clothesline."

Dave led Shep around the evil, strangler clothesline.

"Make a note, Pietro. Buy Miranda an electric clothes dryer," said Shepard. "And a real car."

17 THE MESSAGE

Shepard's calm demeanor hid a volcano of rage when he sat down at the microphone that night. In the two hours since leaving Miranda's half-charred house, his mind had built a dozen scenarios. Each horrified him more than the last.

Miranda might have died in that fire.

Miranda could have been murdered by the knife-wielding arsonist.

Dave could have been sliced in two by that same knife.

If the arsonist had waited five minutes longer, Pietro, Shep, and Dave would not have been home to intervene.

Every house in Minokee could have burned.

The whole forest could have been reduced to charcoal.

Okay, probably not the whole neighborhood or the whole forest. But the most tragic scenarios—death to those he loved—were too deeply within the realm of possibility.

Shep's fury had a target. His enemy had a name, if not yet a face. Iggy had declared war. Bad news for Iggy.

Promptly at 11:00 p.m., Shep hit the button to start his theme music. He waited two seconds then pulled down the music and potted up his mic. Like hot fudge syrup his deep voice flowed from radios across north-central Florida.

"This is Shepard Krausse, and you're listening to Sheep Counters with Shep and Dave on eighty-three point nine, WLOK-FM in Live Oak. We're here to help you light the night. And you fellow sheep counters out there are a vital part of this program. So make some notes about the issues that keep you awake, and let's talk about them. Call us at 877-555-S-H-E-P."

Outside the slanted glass of the control room window, Pietro began answering phones and taking caller information. Inside the control room, Shepard dragged air into his lungs and leaned into the microphone.

"Before we talk with our first caller," he said, "I've got a story of my own to share. It's about a guy named Iggy. Iggy has a lot of power in this state. Iggy has been making a lot of money fixing bids on state construction projects for the last few years. Iggy has been costing us taxpayers a ton of cash.

"That's tax money we paid—sometimes willingly, sometimes not, but we paid—because we know tax money builds schools, maintains and builds roads, builds low-income housing, builds libraries and parks and mass transit systems. And Iggy took our money and lined a dishonest contractor's fat pockets with it. A lot of that cash landed in Iggy's pocket, too.

"Iggy committed fraud upon fraud upon fraud, and he stole from all of us. That was bad enough. But, you see, Iggy is not just a thief. He's also a coward.

"It takes a coward to murder a little old lady because of a letter she wrote or some pictures she might have taken when she was out bird-watching.

"It takes a coward to plant a venomous snake in the path of a blind man.

"And just tonight, a coward set fire to a harmless young lady's home and nearly killed her.

"You've gone too far, Iggy. We've been waiting for you to come forward, turn state's evidence, and redeem yourself by putting an end to the bidding scheme and sending the rich contractor to jail.

"We've waited while you went from conspiracy and fraud to murder and attempted murder and arson. We're through waiting."

The pitch of his voice fell from dark chocolate to black tar pit. Instead of delicious warmth, the sound boiled with menace and danger. Shepard spoke as if whispering into someone's ear, "I'm coming for you, Iggy."

Outside the slanted window, Pietro had gone still, staring at Shep. Then Pietro closed his eyes and shook his head.

"We'll be back with our first caller in just a minute. You're listening to Sheep Counters with Shep and Dave on eighty-three point nine, WLOK-FM, Live Oak. Be right back."

A commercial message replaced his voice on the airwaves. Shep potted down his mic and leaned back in his chair. The next few hours should be very interesting.

18 THE DECISION

The following morning, while Shep and Dave ran their morning route and the Magnolia Street ladies sat on the porch with Miranda and their coffee, two men were talking just a few miles from the houses of Minokee.

Their huge, shiny cars were parked at the end of an old logging road deep in the forest. Headlights glowed in the morning half-light. The men stood between the cars, alone, face to face.

"Reggie," said the contractor in greeting.

"Thanks for coming," said the governor.

"You said it was important. I'm here." The man was emotionless except for the hint of disdain in his eyes when he looked at the governor. His look said, *I own you.*

"We've had a good run," Reggie said. "We've both profited, and so far we've been untouchable. But the handwriting is on the wall now. It's time for us to stop. Go our separate ways."

The contractor nodded, taking in the ideas. "What brought this on?" he asked.

Reggie handed the contractor a compact disc. "Did you hear the Sheep Counter program last night?"

"I don't listen to that crap."

"That's a recording of it," Reggie indicated the disc. "You only need to hear the first three minutes. He's putting his facts together. He may not have any proof yet, but he'll soon have enough circumstantial evidence to get law enforcement interested. If they start digging seriously, they are sure to find enough to ruin us."

"Pssht," the contractor scoffed. "People like us don't go to prison, Reggie. That's what lawyers are for."

Reggie's voice climbed to a higher register. "Sure! The lawyers end up with the money we made, and we end up with no life. I'll lose my career, my family, and my future along with the money. You think *prison* is the worst that can happen? Think again, pal!"

The contractor placed a hand on Reggie's shoulder. The gesture was restraining rather than comforting. "Calm down," he said. "What is the situation exactly, huh? Some conspiracy nut says on the radio that he's gonna rat us out. If he knows so much, why doesn't he just name names? Why doesn't he accuse us? He hasn't done it because he can't. He's got nothing. Don't let him scare you into doing something foolish. That's exactly what he's hoping for."

Reggie took some deep breaths. His voice lowered to near normal. "You don't know Shepard Krausse. He's not a flake. He knows the law, and he'll use it. He'll name the names when he knows he's got enough evidence to defend a civil suit for defamation of character. He'll force us into court, and then all his accusations will be public record. And he's media. He's got media connections. Even if the court rules in our favor, he'll make sure public opinion rules against us. We can be officially, legally innocent, and we'll still be screwed."

The contractor shrugged. "Okay, then. Now that we've identified the problem, I'll take care of it."

"He's my sister's son," said Reggie. "I can't harm him. She'll kill me. I'm not kidding."

"Chill out, my friend. You won't harm anybody. I got this. It's handled. Relax. Go home and have breakfast." The contractor extended his hand in farewell.

Reggie shook hands and nearly bowed. "Okay, I guess. Thanks for coming."

"No problem," said the contractor. "Let's not do it again."

A moment later the two cars rolled quietly away from the clearing, out of the forest, and on to their separate destinations.

19 THE SUPPER

The following evening Miranda returned from work to find Dave sitting patiently beside her driveway. When she emerged from her tiny car, Dave jogged to her and sat, looking into her face. He carried a rolled sheet of paper in his teeth.

"Hey, Dave, sweetie," said Miranda, patting his head and scratching the soft dimple behind his ear. "Is that for me?"

She gently grasped the rolled paper, and Dave released it into her hand. The message, unfurled, read, "Your kitchen is toast. Have dinner with us. Come as you are." It was signed "P., S., & D."

Miranda laughed. "I guess you're my escort?" she said to Dave. "In that case, 'Lead on, McDuff.'"

"Whupf," snuffed Dave, and he began padding toward the back hedge.

"Oh, you don't like Shakespeare. Too pretentious?" said Miranda, following him across the yard.

Moments later the Krausse kitchen door swung open just as Dave and Miranda approached it. "Been listening for you," said Shepard, gesturing for her to enter.

"I appreciate the invitation," she said. "To tell the truth, I hadn't given a thought to what I was going to do about dinner. I keep forgetting I don't have a kitchen. Ooh, what smells so delectable in here?"

"I'ma make you my grandmother's especial *torta rustica*, with super secret ingredient. You gonna love it," Pietro spoke from his place at the stove. He wore a red apron that covered him from armpits to knees.

Miranda translated the Italian words embroidered on the apron: " 'Cooking lasts longer than kissing?' And what, sir chef, do you mean by that, exactly?"

Pietro looked up from the pot he was stirring and grinned at her. "It means if you smart, you don't marry the pretty one," he nodded toward Shepard and winked, "you marry the one who can cook."

"Watch it, buddy," snarled Shepard.

"Calm down, Thor," said Pietro. "We just talkin' about my apron."

"Your apron, my a—"

"Shepard!" Miranda interrupted, feigning outrage. "If you intend to propose to me every time you speak to me, you can hardly complain if someone else does it, too, now can you?" She winked at Pietro.

Shepard opened his mouth as if to argue, then closed it and pulled back a chair for Miranda. "Have a seat, Castor Bean. What can I get you to drink?"

"Thank you," she said, taking her place at the table. As Shep settled her chair, she asked, "What are you two drinking?"

"Iced tea," Shep answered. "We have to leave for work after dinner."

Pietro announced, "Everybody sit! It'sa perfect right now. In ten minutes will be ruined. Sit! Sit!"

"You sit! I'm getting the tea," Shepard said.

"*Velocemente!* I'ma serve the plates!" snapped Pietro.

Shepard said something rude in Italian. Pietro ignored him. Miranda laughed. Dave went to his waiting food dish and sat beside it.

....

As they consumed Pietro's culinary masterpiece—which indeed it was—they enjoyed talking in first one language, then another. Miranda held her own in four of the languages, though her accent was admittedly imperfect. Pietro and

Shepard knew a smattering of Russian, Turkish, even Hebrew, but when they discovered Miranda wasn't keeping up, they quickly changed to a tongue with which she was familiar.

They were discussing the mysteries of the game of cricket when Shep suddenly raised a hand for silence.

"Hear that?" he said.

"What is it?" asked Pietro.

"That car," said Shepard. "Listen."

They stilled their forks and listened. A car was idling somewhere on Orchid Street. The neighborhood was otherwise quiet.

"Whose car is that?" asked Shepard.

"Who knows?" said Pietro, resuming his dinner. "You think I can tell from just hearing a car that it belongs to a certain person?"

"Come on, Pietro. There aren't that many cars on Orchid Street. There aren't that many cars in all of Minokee. Nobody around here has a car that sounds like that."

Pietro shook his head. "You justa showing off in front of the pretty lady."

"I am not," Shep turned toward Miranda. "Bean, I am not showing off. Look, your car sounds like a sewing machine with its teeny engine. Martha's car rattles. Mr. Barren's car squeaks. Bernice's old caddy rumbles like a steam locomotive." He turned toward Pietro. "Our car purrs like a kitten, because you baby it all the time. But that car," he gestured toward the outside, "that car sounds like a biker gang. It doesn't belong in this neighborhood."

Miranda put a hand on Shepard's wrist. "Somebody has company, that's all. You have a dinner guest. They have one, too. Don't let it worry you."

Shepard smiled and patted her hand. "I'm not worried. I just noticed, is all."

"You justa showing off, is all," muttered Pietro.

"Stop it," Miranda said with a chuckle. "You were explaining to me about cricket."

With that, Pietro resumed the conversation they had interrupted. Their pleasant dinner continued without further distractions.

After the meal, Miranda sipped coffee at the table while Pietro and Shep cleaned up the kitchen. Dinner had been extraordinary. In fact, Miranda thought she had never enjoyed such superb food in such marvelous company in her life. If this was an everyday meal at the Krausse household, these friends were very special indeed.

"You have this down to a science," she said, watching them wash, dry, and put away the dishes and utensils.

"Years of practice," said Shep.

"I teach him how to run a kitchen," said Pietro.

Shep elbowed Pietro. "Liar! Your grandmother taught me," he turned toward Miranda. "His grandmother taught me."

"Hah! You forget that I teach my grandmother!" Pietro quipped, elbowing Shep in return.

Miranda laughed. "Clearly, you've known each other for a very long time. What was Shepard like in high school?"

"Perfect!" said Shepard.

"Tall," said Pietro. "And skinny and insecure and a poor student. Everything I was not, that's what he was."

"No," inserted Shep.

"And he had no, how can I say, ... skills, no ... finesse with the girls," Pietro continued.

"What girls? There were no girls!" Shep turned to Miranda. "There were no girls. It was an all-boys boarding school. No girls."

"There are girls in the town," Pietro insisted. "Plenty of girls, who admire the dark, handsome Italian with the hypnotizing charm."

"Oh, right, hypnotizing charm. I suppose you're referring to yourself, Harry Houdini?"

"Houdini? Houdini was an escape artist. I no want to escape from pretty girls."

"Spare me," muttered Shep.

"Fortunately, I take pity on this pathetic oaf—"

"Pathetic oaf!"

"—and I give him lessons in romance," Pietro boasted.

"Do you realize how awful that sounds?!" Shep said. He turned toward Miranda, "He did not teach me. Nobody had to teach me." He turned toward Pietro. "You did not teach me, you self-proclaimed little Wop Romeo."

"You Norse Neanderthal," said Pietro.

Through it all they washed and rinsed, dried and stacked, and never missed a beat. Miranda laughed until tears ran down her cheeks. Dave dozed under the table with his head on Miranda's feet. He had heard it all before.

"So, that's our story," Shep said. "What was school like for you, Castor Bean?"

Miranda was quiet a moment, looking into her coffee cup.

"Oh, you know. Good grades. Teachers liked me; students not so much. People couldn't remember my name. Nobody mistreated me or bullied me. Mostly people were unaware of me. Never had my picture in the yearbook. But it was all good. School was fine." She looked down at her feet. "What was school like for you, Dave?"

"Whupf," Dave snuffled.

"He's too modest," said Shepard. "Dave graduated first in his class, was captain of the Frisbee team, and dated the most beautiful poodle babe on campus."

Pietro chimed in, "Dave is so smart, when he graduate they hire him as a professor for two semesters."

Miranda laughed. She finished her coffee and rose to hand her empty cup to Pietro. He added it to his dishwater.

"Thank you for a wonderful meal and for the, um, unusual conversation," she said. "I need to get home and get to bed early, and you two need to get off to work soon."

Shep put down his drying towel and walked her to the kitchen door. "Will you stay with Martha again tonight?" he asked.

"Oh, no, I'm fine at my place," she assured him. "Martha spent the day getting doors and windows secured and some of the kitchen mess swept away. She's kept me on the phone all day with progress reports. We have wonderful neighbors here, don't we?"

"I certainly have a wonderful neighbor," he agreed. He opened the door for her and kissed her on the forehead. "Be safe. Sleep well."

"You, too. Thanks again," she said, and she began walking homeward.

"Oh, Bean?" he called after her.

"Yes?"

"Will you marry me?" he called.

She laughed. "Not tonight, Shepard." She kept walking.

"Okay. G'night," he called, and shut the door.

Minokee exploded twenty minutes later.

20 THE HUNTED

Miranda had removed her shoes and laid out her work clothing for the next morning. She was covering her charred kitchen with spare bed sheets when a blast of noise and light shook the house and knocked her to her knees.

An echoing muffled roar followed the first boom. The initial bright light subsided to a wavering red-gold glow emanating from Orchid Street.

Miranda blinked and pulled in air, but she choked and coughed on suspended dust and ash stirred by the explosion. Sputtering and gasping, she pushed herself to her feet. The flames and smoke were concentrated beyond the roof of her rear-yard neighbor. She knew—but tried desperately to deny—that Shepard Krausse's front yard was on fire.

She fumbled into the flip-flops beside the door. In a millisecond she raced through the rear hedge. The red glow blossomed higher into the air beyond the Krausse rooftop. Neighbors' doors slammed, dogs barked, people shouted as all Minokee rushed to help. Some woman was screaming hysterically; Miranda decided the voice was her own.

She careened around the side of the house and froze in shock. At the curb a massive conflagration devoured twisted, blackened pieces of Pietro's car. In the street beyond, shadows of frantic neighbors fought the fire with buckets, garden hoses, and kitchen fire extinguishers. People shouted into cell phones and at each other. What air was not sucked away by the holocaust was searing to the lungs. A wall of unbearable heat shoved would-be rescuers back from the white-hot steel skeleton of the car.

Squinting into the blinding glare, Miranda made out a silhouette no one else had yet seen: a body on the lawn, and it was on fire.

"Shepard!" she screamed. "Shepard!"

She ran and threw her body across the burning one. She rolled him in the grass, she beat out flames with her hands, ripped off her blouse and skirt and smothered the fire. His pant legs were shredded and black. Now in her underwear, Miranda wrapped her singed outer clothing around his calves and leaped to grasp his wrists and drag him toward safety. A gnarled, claw like hand covered Miranda's hand. She jumped and screamed.

"Let me help!" shouted Martha Cleary over the hideous cacophony surrounding them.

Miranda pulled one arm and Martha the other. Together they heaved the big man to and through the front door of his house. Martha slammed the door, blocking out most of the heat and light, but the two women had no trouble seeing each other's terrified faces in the fire's glare through the windows. They slumped onto the floor beside the unconscious Shepard. Martha wore pin curls, a bathrobe, and ruined pink chenille bedroom slippers. Miranda wore bra, panties, half-slip, one flip-flop, and a coating of soot marred by tear tracks down her face. She made no sound and took no notice as tiny salty drops fell from her chin.

"Gonna take the Rescue a bit ta git out here," said Martha, hauling herself to her feet. "Better get some cool water on these burns." She gestured to Shepard's lower legs encased in Miranda's erstwhile clothing. "I'll git a bowl of cool water from the kitchen."

"I'll get some towels," Miranda said with a sniff. She wiped her chin absently on the back of her hand as she rose and went to find a linen closet.

Moments later the women were again seated alongside the man who lay facedown, silent, on the floor. Gently they lifted away the clothing on his calves, placed towels beneath him, and began drizzling cooling water over his reddened skin.

Outside someone shouted, "Everybody get back! Get back!" Unable to put out the flames, neighbors retreated to what they hoped was a safe distance. Some wept. Some joined hands and prayed. Everyone lurched backward when a second, smaller explosion blasted new flames high into the air.

"Prolly the gas tank," said Martha when Miranda pulled back and squeaked with alarm. Miranda took a deep breath, let it out, and resumed the gentle rinsing of the man's burns. Martha never broke rhythm. For a minute they worked in silence, with the decreasing glow and fading fiery roar coming to them through the closed front door and the living room windows.

Miranda cleared her throat and asked hoarsely, "Martha?"

"Yeah, darlin'."

"Wh-where is Dave? Where is Pietro? Is, is somebody helping them?"

Martha took a couple of calming breaths before she answered, as kindly as she could, "I think they're still in the car."

"Oh, God! Dear God, have mercy!" Miranda whispered.

Shepard groaned. His shoulders tensed, and he turned his head toward Miranda.

She wiped his face with a cool, damp cloth. "Shhhhh," she said, leaning near his ear. "It's all right. You're gonna be all right."

His eyes were closed, but his lips moved. Miranda said, "What, Shep? What do you want?"

He worked harder, and this time they heard him. "Dave," he rasped. "Where's Dave?"

No one answered.

Unconsciousness reclaimed him.

The next fifteen minutes dragged on for decades. Miranda looked at her watch, thumped it with her fingers, held it to her ear, certain that it had stopped. The noise outside had subsided. The fire had decreased from open flames to glowing edges of unrecognizable shapes. Most neighbors had gone home; only a few waited for the police and fire/rescue vehicles.

Miranda and Martha continued rinsing Shepard's calves. Martha declared the burns were superficial and limited to his lower legs. Miranda examined them closely and agreed.

When Shepard stirred and opened his eyes, the women helped him stand and move to the nearby sofa. They propped his feet on an ottoman and draped wet towels over his shins to cool his burns. Martha fetched a glass of water, and Miranda fed it to him.

Silently, Miranda thanked God that Shepard could not see the devastation outside his front window. She could not keep her eyes off it. She yearned to see—and at the same time prayed not to see—the shapes of a man and a large dog inside the twisted metal.

Shepard had lost his sunglasses in the blast, and his blue eyes stared unblinking into middle space. His head ached— from concussion, he surmised—and his calves felt like the time he had fallen asleep on the white-sand beach at Destin. Unforgettable second-degree sunburn. At least this time it was only his legs, not the backside of his entire body.

Martha went outside to confer with neighbors and watch for the authorities. Shepard and Miranda sat in silence.

"Would you like me to call your mother?" Miranda asked softly.

He shook his head carefully, as if it hurt to move. They sat isolated in their own thoughts a little longer. Then Shepard said, "Bean, I need to call Carlo."

"Carlo?" she said. "Who is Carlo? Never mind. Doesn't matter. Do you have his number?"

"It's in my phone. But I have no idea where my phone is."

"It's on your coffee table. I found it in your pocket."

He groaned and dropped his face into his hands.

She rose, retrieved the phone, and when he sat up again placed it in his hand. He held it. He thumbed it on, then flicked it off again. He lifted it toward Miranda.

"I can't," he said. "Would you?"

"Sure," she said, taking the phone. She turned on the device and scrolled through the contacts directory. She found "Carlo" in the directory and activated the call button. "It's ringing," she said. "What do you want me to say?"

Shep cleared his throat. "Tell him his brother has been murdered," he said, then seemed to choke. He coughed and continued, "And I'm sorry. I'm so sorry. I'm so sorry." He clamped his jaws shut and swallowed hard. Tears pooled in his eerie blue eyes and rolled unchecked down into his beard.

Miranda steeled herself for the conversation, and when Carlo answered she was able to speak almost normally. His Italian accent was nearly identical to Pietro's, and that tore at her heart. Still, she managed to introduce herself as a friend and neighbor of Shepard's and to tell him Shepard's message more-or-less verbatim.

Carlo was quiet a moment. Miranda put the call on Speaker and held it between herself and Shepard.

"Who?" said Carlo. The single word spoke sorrow, fury, determination, and inescapable vengeance.

Shepard managed to force from his constricted throat: "Iggy. Has to be Iggy."

"And madam?" said the voice of vengeance.

Miranda's brow furrowed in confusion.

Shepard answered, more strongly now, "I am certain madam knows nothing of this. She is not part of it. I caused this, Carlo. Pietro warned me, but I didn't listen. I thought I was risking only myself. I should have realized there was as much danger to the people around me." Shep's chest heaved with his weeping. "I'm sorry," he rasped.

For a few seconds Miranda heard only Shepard sobbing. She slipped her arm across his wide shoulders and hugged him.

Finally, Carlo spoke again. If Death could speak, it would be in that voice. "Is not for you be sorry. Is for Iggy. Iggy will be the most sorry." He disconnected.

Shepard stared straight ahead, gaining control of himself. Miranda's hand slid soothingly back and forth across his shoulders. Only eighteen minutes had passed since life had changed forever in a ball of fire. In another ten minutes the outside world would arrive with flashing lights and helping hands.

Suddenly Shepard stiffened. "Hear that?" he whispered.

Miranda wiped at her wet cheeks and listened. Outside, a car approached and idled to a stop near the wreckage. A man called out, "What the hell happened here?!"

"Car fire," a neighbor shouted back, in a tone that also said, *as any fool can see.*

"Damn! Anybody hurt?" the newcomer yelled.

"One got out," Martha Cleary shouted. "You lost or somethin'?"

The man in the car told a fast story of old maps, bad lighting, and wrong turns. He asked how to get back to the interstate. Someone outside seemed to be giving directions.

"It's the same car, isn't it!" Miranda whispered, as if the strangers might hear and discover them. "The one you heard during dinner!"

"Now we know what they were doing in Minokee," Shepard said.

"And now they know someone survived," said Miranda.

"Yeah," said Shepard. "They're gonna want to finish the job for sure." He stood and held out his hand to her. "Bean, we gotta go. *Velocemente!* C'mon!"

She put her hand in his, he pulled her with him, and they headed out his back door toward the break in the hedge.

"But we can't run from them! You're hurt," Miranda protested. "Can't we just hide—if not here, then in my house—until the police and paramedics get here? It won't be much longer now."

"Trust me, Castor Bean. Those guys intend to be finished up and long gone before the police get here. I don't suppose you've replaced Phyllis' shotgun that was stolen?"

"No, I—"

"Doesn't matter. We may be unarmed, but we're not dead, and we're on our own turf. Feeling woodsy?"

"What?" Miranda was running as fast as she could in one flip-flop, but when they had crossed Shep's yard, the hedge, and her own back yard, she dug in her heels and pulled him to a stop. Panting, she told him, "I need shoes!"

She led him into her house and left him fidgeting in the living room. Dashing to her bedroom closet, she stamped into a pair of loafers at the same time she whipped a denim sundress off a hangar and over her head. She refused to run for her life wearing only her undies. Sure, Shepard couldn't see her, but there might be ambulance drivers, the police, the (ick!) undertaker. Not to mention the murderers sure to be pursuing them. She needed clothing and whatever dignity it afforded,

"Let's go!" she said, grabbed Shep's hand, and trotted out the door. Crossing her front yard, she asked, "Where to? My car!"

"No, they'd follow us. We'd be a teeny-weeny sitting duck in your clown car. Just run. Straight across the road from your front gate, turn left. Follow the edge of the asphalt for a hundred twenty-five paces. There's a deer trail into the Cypress."

She hesitated a half-second, then pulled him with her across the road. He took the lead as they turned left and counted steps. At the designated spot, he stopped and turned right. "See it?" he asked.

Night had settled down in the Little Cypress forest like a cat settling into a nap. Miranda took a step left, then right, before discerning a grayness amid the blackness. She stepped into the gray and found herself on a narrow dirt path through the dense undergrowth. "It's here!" she said.

He stepped past her to take the lead, and off they went into the scrub.

"You really know your way around in here?" she gasped, tripping over a thick strangler fig tendril. Shep lifted her one-handed before she hit the ground. He set her on her feet, steadied her, then resumed their trek.

"I've been exploring and camping and bird-watching in here every summer I can remember. Phyllis brought me. She said if I could learn to survive in here, I'd be fine anywhere."

Miranda felt him step over something and barely managed to get over the same log herself without scraping her shins, stubbing her toes, or falling flat on her face. "It's so dark in here!" she said.

"Bean, it's always dark—and not just in here," he said.

"Oh, yeah," she said. She followed him to the left and back again to the trail. He avoided a puddle. She drenched one foot in it. "Wait a minute! 'Bird-watching?' Seriously?"

Moonlight skittered across his white-toothed grin as they passed through openings between trees. "Thought you'd catch that one quicker. You must be distracted by something."

"Kinda," she panted, clenching his hand and trotting to keep pace as he dodged obstacles and ducked low branches. Then her foot plunged into a hole where solid ground should have been. She clamped one hand over her mouth to stifle her involuntary cry.

Shep froze. "What!?"

"I fell in a hole," she whispered, using his hand to pull herself out of the knee-deep, sandy trap. "Huge hole," she said, then squeaked, "It's not a snake hole is it!?"

"How huge?" he asked.

"A foot across. I fell in up to my knee, but it could be deeper."

"Armadillo. Big one." He pulled her after him as he began moving again. "Don't worry, they're almost never man-eaters."

"Dude, if you're trying to scare me, you're way too late."

They had penetrated about two hundred yards into the woods when Shepard stopped and about-faced. "Look back at the road now," he said.

Miranda turned, placed her back against his torso, and peered through the dark. "I see two lights bobbing around. Looks like they're walking down Magnolia Street."

"Toward us or away?" he asked.

"Away."

"Can you see their car?"

"No."

"No flashing emergency vehicles yet?"

"Sorry, no."

"Don't be sorry, Bean. This is a great adventure. Smell the roses."

"I'm too busy smelling the psycho killers," she said. "Uh-oh."

"What?"

"They turned around just beyond Bernice's house. They're coming back this way."

"Okay, then," said Shep. "Time to play mama bear and baby bear, Castor Bean. How are you at climbing trees?"

"Please tell me that's a rhetorical question."

He pulled her farther along the trail. Soon he began raking his free hand across the bark of the large trees they passed. When he found the tree he wanted, he stopped and turned to Miranda. That was when she realized he had been counting his steps since they had left the pavement. He knew right where they were, and he knew what he would find there.

"You're gonna be the baby bear," he told her. "You're gonna climb as far as you can up this tree, then mama bear's gonna climb up behind you and protect you from the mean old hunters."

"I'm not sure, but I think there's a sexist remark in there somewhere," said Miranda.

He pointed up into the tree. "Think you can do it?"

"Anything you can do, I can do better. Maybe," she said, looking up through tangled branches where a faint dusting of moonlight was the only thing showing the way.

Shep placed her hands on a sturdy branch with a U-shaped dip close to the tree's trunk. "I'll give you a boost," he said. He placed his hands at her waist and easily lifted her above his head. She straddled the low branch.

"Movin' on up," she sang beneath her breath as she gripped higher boughs, got her feet under her, and began climbing from one limb to the next.

Shep listened to her progress. When he thought she was well out of his way, he pulled himself onto the low branch. He moved only a few limbs higher, then settled himself and went still.

Miranda heard him stop. Following his example, she nested silently where she was.

She watched.

He listened.

A minute later, one of the distant flashlights turned off the road in their direction.

"They found the trail," she whispered.

"Hang tight," he breathed.

The treed humans froze so completely that the owls, crickets, and tree frogs resumed their nightly noises as if no *Homo sapiens* had joined them—arboreal or otherwise.

A lizard walked onto Miranda's hand, and she wondered if a heart attack would cause her to fall or cause her dead muscles to cling permanently to the tree. She kept her vocal cords silent, but her mind was screeching maniacally. Just when she had decided to faint and let nature take its course, the lizard waddled away, slithering its long slinky tail across her skin. She began breathing again but promised herself a good, satisfying vomit when this was all over.

Her mind traveled to the lower branch where Shep waited. If she had not known better, she would have thought herself alone in the tree. He made no sound, no twitch. He had to be in terrible pain, squatting in a tree with fresh burns covering his lower legs. She was sure he had a headache and most likely a concussion, and she prayed he wouldn't get dizzy or pass out and fall.

When thoughts of Dave and Pietro crossed Shep's mind, he shoved them ruthlessly aside. Survival first; heartrending agony later. First, take necessary steps to secure for himself (and Miranda) a future; later, try to imagine a future without—he refused even to name them in his mind. His lost ones must remain a black void for now, or he would shut down completely, leaving Miranda in the merciless hands of killers.

Miranda's brain traveled a similar circuit, except that she had the disadvantage of seeing over and over again the conflagration and shifting shapes among the flames. She had to view repeatedly the moment when she realized the burning debris on the lawn was actually Shepard. She tried to name the state capitals, the presidents and vice presidents in order, the major Dewey Decimal categories, anything to force herself to visualize something, anything, besides hellish death.

The first flashlight was approaching slowly. The man had to be feeling his way along the foot-wide trail. She could see the light bobble when he stumbled and nearly fell. She imagined she could hear him cursing as he scraped against tree bark or craggy oolitic rock outcroppings.

Miranda prayed for a dramatic entrance by a Florida panther, a razor-tusked wild boar, a black bear in a very bad mood, a rabid coyote, or even a blue heron with a stabbing beak. But if they were waiting in the wings, they never took the stage to rescue the damsel from the villains. She expected little help from turtles, insects, reptiles, and amphibians – all of them present in great numbers but ineffective as crime fighters. Where was a Chupacabra when you needed one?

The second man had turned onto the trail many yards behind the first. He seemed to progress more easily with the advantage of the first man's light ahead. Now two lights drew white arcs on the rough ground and bobbed inexorably toward the tree that scarcely hid the two fugitives. If a hunter turned his flashlight upward, Shep and Miranda were doomed.

Miranda's hands ached from clutching the bough above her. Her back muscles cramped from staying bent in an awkward crouch. Her thighs burned and her calves went numb from squatting, balanced on a narrow branch. The urge to move, to adjust, to ease the pain was unrelenting. And with every second, the nearest hunter was closer and more likely to hear any rustle of leaf or clothing.

The first man was just four yards from the tree, now, and Miranda could see from the backwash of his flashlight that he had drawn a handgun and kept it pointing everywhere the light swept.

The other man was still many yards away, but Miranda felt certain he was armed as well. Both men had already committed murder once tonight. They had everything to gain and nothing to lose by exterminating Shep and Miranda.

The forest denizens went silent. Miranda's muscles screamed for relief. Below her, she felt rather than heard Shepard draw his strength together for flight or fight.

The first hunter was now three yards away. Two yards. Shep launched from the tree, hanging by his arms like a great ape, slamming both feet into the gunman's chest.

Both men fell.

Both grunted with pain.

The flashlight flew into the bush.

Oily blackness coated everything.

The gun disappeared into the undergrowth.

Miranda jumped, slipped, clambered, and swung down from the tree. Two heavy forms grappled, grunting and panting, on the ground. Miranda tried to reach the fallen flashlight, but bloodthirsty thorns and thick vines held her off.

Dust rose from the ground as the men scrambled blindly after the missing gun. The battle was as quiet as it was deadly. From far down the trail, the second hunter could perceive only that the light had gone out.

"What's the deal?!" he bellowed through the trees. "Didja see 'em?! Carney! Do ya see 'em?"

The one called Carney didn't answer. His throat was beneath Shep's iron forearm. Shep strained to close the distance between his arm and the dirt, crushing Carney's larynx, esophagus, and windpipe. Carney would not be talking or breathing ever again.

Miranda stood by, praying silently and actually trying, for a change, to be invisible. Shep remained hunched over his foe after the man went still.

The remaining gunman reacted to his partner's sudden ominous silence by charging forward, careless of his footing. Eager to kill.

Shep reached toward Miranda. She helped him rise stiffly, painfully.

No light.

No gun.

They faced the oncoming hunter.

He was close.

They were spent.

It would end here.

Abruptly, the killer swung around the nearest bend in the trail and pinned Shepard dead-on in his light. He smiled and raised his pistol. Miranda screamed, "No!" and flung herself across Shep, arms wrapped tight around his ribs, with her back to the gunman.

Shep was trying to pry the female shield off his chest while, at the same time, struggling to turn them both so that his body was between Miranda and the murderer.

A shot blasted the night.

Everyone froze for a second and a half. Shepard came out of his stupor and clutched Miranda to him.

"Oh, God help us! Miranda! Miranda!"

Miranda had closed her eyes and waited for the pain. When she realized she was uninjured, her first fear was that Shepard had replaced her in the shooter's sights.

She wrapped her arms about his waist and ran her hands over his big frame as far and as fast as she could. She didn't even think of stifling her sobs, and between each one she cried out some version of, "I'm fine. I'm all right. Are you hurt? Are you bleeding?"

Then they both heard a dull thud like an overstuffed duffle falling off a baggage cart. Miranda turned her head and opened her eyes. The gunman lay facedown in the dirt, illuminated by his flashlight on the ground beside him.

"Miranda!" demanded Shepard. "Answer me!"

She swallowed her sobs as reality penetrated her hysteria. On a grateful impulse, she lifted herself on tiptoes and gave him a short but solid kiss on the lips. "I'm okay," she breathed. "Are you hurt?"

"No worse than before." He hugged her to him, then grasped her shoulders and pushed her back an arm's length. "What did you think you were doing?! Are you crazy!? You could've been killed!"

Martha Cleary stepped into the white oval cast by the dead man's fallen flashlight. Her rifle hung from the crook of her elbow. "Ain't gone be no more killin' tonight," she said. She picked up the flashlight and shone it across one limp body and then the other. "Them fellers picked the wrong place ta do their mischief in. We takes care of our own in Minokee."

Engines rumbled on the asphalt beyond the trees, and blue lights flashed between the black shadows of palmetto bushes, southern pines, strangler figs, stopper trees, cypress, and live oaks.

"'Bout time they got here," Martha groused. She gave Shep and Miranda a thorough inspection, heads to toes, with her light. "Y'all better stay here. I'll hightail it out there and bring back the paramedics."

"Oh, Martha!" was all Miranda could get out.

"Don't you dare thank me, chile!" the old lady bellowed as she moved briskly down the trail toward the police and fire vehicles.

Shep and Miranda leaned on each other and concentrated on breathing in and breathing out. When their heart rates had settled into less than a full gallop, and breathing had become less of a chore, Shep said, "Bean, I'm sorry but I gotta ... sit d–."

He passed out mid-word. Miranda braced herself against the trunk of their tree and managed to lower him to the ground without injuring either of them further.

Minutes later four paramedics with large lights, medical supplies, and a stretcher rushed toward her on the trail. She couldn't remember, later, what was said or by whom. She only knew that Shepard was being airlifted to Montgomery Memorial Hospital, and that she was staying by his side come hell or high water or imperious mothers or dishonest politicians or would-be murderers.

Miranda had appointed herself the new Dave.

21 THE VENDETTA

Governor Reginald Jackson Montgomery drove his Jaguar coupe past the security guard at the entrance to his estate. Reggie maintained token residence in the governor's mansion, but he frequently spent time at the family home midway between Tallahassee and Live Oak. In truth, Reggie's house was nicer than the governor's mansion, but he liked to keep the public unaware of that.

It was after midnight, but that was standard for a man who attended evening dinners and late meetings before making the long drive out to the Montgomery compound. Security was tight, so Reggie had no qualms about arriving alone at this hour.

Surprise lifted his eyebrows when he saw his sister's limousine parked near the five-car garage behind the main house. He certainly wanted no aggravation from Hermione tonight. She had made herself painfully clear the last time they met. Her baby boy was off limits. Okay. Reggie had passed the word to his confederates. Nothing more to say.

When Reggie emerged from his Jag, however, he was greeted not by his sister but by her chauffeur.

"Carlo?" said the governor.

"Yes. I am Carlo. And you, I believe, are Iggy."

The governor laughed nervously. "Wherever did you hear that name? What's this about? Where's Mrs. Montgomery-Krausse?"

119

"I hear about Iggy from madam. She don't tell me, but I hear. She was little, little girl. She can no say 'Reggie,' so she say 'Iggy.' Is true, yes?"

"Wow, that's been a long, long time ago. But you're right. She called me Iggy until I finished grammar school. What's going on, Carlo? Did my sister send you?"

"My brother send me."

"I don't understand." Reggie was sweating. Carlo's brother was with Shepard Krausse. If Pietro sent Carlos to confront Reggie, something must have happened to Reggie's troublesome nephew. The governor backed away until the Jag pressed his backside, and he could go no further. Confusion and fear warred for supremacy in his face.

Carlo lifted an old double-barreled shotgun he had been holding behind one leg. He leveled it at Reggie's mid-section and BOOM, fired one barrel. A red crater opened in Reggie's diaphragm.

"That'sa for my brother, Pietro," Carlo said calmly. Then BOOM, he fired the second barrel. "And that'sa for Dave." A second, overlapping crater appeared, centered on what might have been Reggie's heart, if he'd ever had one.

Expression faded from Reggie's face and the light went out in Reggie's eyes. Carlo walked calmly back to the limousine, got in, and started the engine.

Reggie's body slid slowly down the side of the Jaguar and came to rest on the pavement. A wide crimson path glinted on the door of the car, from the window to the rocker panel. Carlo didn't see it. By that time, the security guard was waving Mrs. Montgomery-Krausse's limousine out of the gate. The guard in his air-conditioned gatehouse never heard a sound from the far-off garage.

22 THE RENAISSANCE

Miranda dozed in a waiting room chair on the fourth floor of Montgomery Memorial Hospital. She didn't hear the bell of the arriving elevator, but she woke suddenly at the sound of her name. A cloud of disorientation and fatigue lifted gradually, and she recognized the two people standing before her.

"Where is he? I want to see him," the imposing woman said.

"He's sleeping," said Miranda. "We can see him at noon, when they wake him to eat something."

"I'll see him now," the woman said. "I'm his mother."

Miranda pushed against the arms of the chair, slowly raising her body upright. She faced the woman like a badger squared off to battle a bison. She was still covered in soot, dirt, sweat, and even blood, from the preceding night. She looked like an extra in a zombie apocalypse film.

"Mrs. Montgomery-Krausse," Miranda said, bristling with authority and confidence, "Shepard had a horrible, tragic night. He will recover. But he needs rest in order to heal. He is going to sleep until it is medically advisable to wake him, and he will receive visitors when it is medically and emotionally advisable for him to receive them. I called you because you are his mother. As such, you are welcome to wait here until the staff directs us to enter Shepard's room. If you try to enter his room before that time, I will personally restrain you and, if necessary, incapacitate you until security guards arrive to take you away. Shepard needs your love and reassurance at the appropriate time. He does not need—and will not be subjected to—your grandstanding, officiousness, overprotective hovering, or interference. I believe you have the mental acuity to comprehend what I am telling you, do you not?"

Hermione Montgomery-Krausse stared at Miranda. Hermione shifted her vintage Chanel handbag from one gloved hand to the other and back again. Her mouth opened as if to speak, then closed. With her lips pressed together, Hermione dropped her eyes from Miranda's face. Then Shepard's mother walked around Miranda and took a seat in one of the uncomfortable waiting-room chairs. Hermione had never seen the zombie apocalypse, but she knew a scary woman when she met one.

Miranda turned to the man in black who accompanied Mrs. Montgomery-Krausse. "Good morning, Hanson."

"Good morning, miss," said Hanson, with rather more energy than he had expended on Miranda in the past. "May I get anything for yourself or for madam?"

"I'm dying for coffee, please. I believe Mrs. Montgomery-Krausse would prefer a cup of tea."

"Right away, miss," said Hanson with a slight bow. He caught the next elevator and left the women alone.

Miranda eased down into her chair. She lowered her chin to her chest and closed her eyes.

Hermione waited, looking straight ahead. After several minutes, she spoke to Miranda without looking her way. "Thank you for telephoning me."

"You love your son," Miranda said weakly. "You needed to know."

Hermione waited, then said, "They truly meant to kill Shepard?"

"They tried their best, yes."

"Does Shepard know about his friend and about the... about his dog?"

"He knows. That's the worst of it for him, I think. Physically, he's strong; he'll bounce back quickly. Emotionally ... who knows?"

Hermione looked at Miranda and evaluated her condition. Leaves and twigs clung to her hair. Bruises dotted her arms and legs, scratches and patterns of dried blood crisscrossed her face, neck, hands, and feet. Her skin was soot-stained, her dress ragged and dirty, and she wore only one shoe.

"Forgive me, my dear, but you need to go home, get a bath, and have a rest, yourself," said Hermione, not unkindly.

Miranda's eyes flew open and her chin jerked up stubbornly. "I'm not leaving," she said.

The women stared into one another's eyes. Miranda's eyes showed no hatred, no anger, no rancor. They also promised no placating, no fear, no backing down.

Hermione blinked first. She admitted to herself, if not to anyone else, that she respected Miranda's commitment to Shepard's wellbeing. Hermione also knew that Miranda had saved Shepard's life. Indeed, they seemed to have saved one another.

"Miss Ogilvy," Hermione said, "if I can arrange for fresh clothing and a room here where you can shower and dress, will you make use of it?"

Miranda examined Hermione's face and found something new there. "Yes," said Miranda, nodding. "I would appreciate that very much." Miranda extended her right hand toward Shepard's mother.

Hermione removed her glove and clasped Miranda's hand. "I'll call my assistant and have her make the arrangements," Hermione said.

When Hanson returned with coffee and tea for the ladies, he found Miranda dozing in her chair and Hermione talking earnestly and efficiently on her phone. Hanson placed the beverages on a table near the chairs, then he took a seat across the room and settled down to wait.

Ninety minutes later a prim middle-aged woman in a conservative business suit stepped off the elevator and approached Mrs. Montgomery-Krausse.

"Yes, Rebecca?" Hermione said.

"Everything is ready, madam. Family suite three-E. Here is the key." Rebecca handed an electronic key card to

Hermione. Hermione waved it aside and directed Rebecca toward Miranda.

"Pardon?" said Miranda, opening her eyes to find the key card thrust at her.

"The hospital keeps a few suites for families of VIP patients," said Hermione. "This is Rebecca. She will escort you to the suite we have reserved. Rebecca has purchased clothing and toiletries for you. Go. Shower and dress. Take a nap. If you need anything, Rebecca will get it for you."

Miranda's eyes widened. Her mouth fell open. She accepted the key card and murmured "Thank you" at Rebecca. Then she looked at Hermione with suspicion. "You aren't getting rid of me so you can sneak into Shepard's room, are you?"

Instead of responding to Miranda, the older woman addressed the butler, who sat across the waiting room.

"Hanson!"

"Yes, madam."

"I order you to prevent me from entering my son's hospital room unless and until I am accompanied there by Miss Ogilvy. I grant you immunity from prosecution or reprisal should you be required to use physical force to accomplish this. Do you acknowledge and accept this directive?"

"Yes, madam."

Hermione looked at Miranda. "You see? Hanson will not permit me to violate your ban on visitors. Rest assured that Hanson holds Shepard in very high esteem and will do whatever is necessary to protect him—even from me. Now, go with Rebecca."

Miranda looked from Hermione to Hanson to Rebecca and back to Hermione. "Thank you," Miranda said. "You're very kind." Miranda stood and gestured to Rebecca to lead the way. Before boarding the elevator, Miranda turned again toward Hermione and said, "I'll be back before noon."

After the elevator departed, carrying Rebecca and Miranda away, Hanson left his chair and crossed the room. He sat down beside Mrs. Montgomery-Krausse. "A formidable young lady," he said.

"Indeed," said Hermione.

"She reminds me of someone," said Hanson.

"Don't be impertinent, Hanson."

"Of course not, madam."

. . . .

The VIP family suites at Montgomery Memorial Hospital were modest but well appointed. They consisted of a small sitting room, comfortable bedroom, and roomy bathroom. Miranda moved like a sleepwalker through the motions of undressing and stepping into the shower. She emerged shampooed and scrubbed and wrapped in a terry cloth bath sheet. She entered the bedroom to find expensive underwear laid out on the bed and three stunning summer dresses hanging on the closet door.

"Madam guessed at the sizes, miss," said Rebecca from the sitting room doorway. "I purchased a size smaller and a size larger in case these do not fit. I'll unpack the other boxes for you if you need them. Just let me know."

Miranda fingered the beautiful undergarments and glanced at the size on the labels. "These should be fine," she murmured, thinking, *they must've cost more than I make in a month!*

Rebecca said, "Madam's stylist is awaiting our call, miss, when you're ready for him to do your hair and makeup."

"That won't be necessary," Miranda said. *I can braid my own hair, and I don't wear makeup.* "But thank you for the offer."

"My pleasure, miss. Do you require assistance with your ensemble?"

"My ensemble? Oh! My clothes, you mean? Ah, no, no thank you. I can, ah, I can get dressed. Thank you."

"Of course, miss. I'll be right outside if you need me." Rebecca backed out of the room and closed the door.

Miranda went to sort through the dresses on the closet door. The colors and fabrics were exquisite. The labels were all from big name designers. "Gee whiz gosh golly holy moley!" she whispered. "Cinderella Ogilvy."

A quarter-hour later Miranda stepped out of the bedroom into the sitting room. Rebecca looked up from a stack of shoeboxes she seemed to be sorting on the coffee table. "You look lovely, miss," said Rebecca.

"Thank you," said Miranda. "It's a really nice outfit. I think it would look better if I wore shoes, though."

"The shoes have just arrived, miss," Rebecca replied, gesturing to the boxes on the coffee table. "I used your old shoe to gauge the size. There are several styles for you to choose from."

"Thank you ... again," said Miranda. She looked around the sitting room and through the door into the bedroom. "What happened to my clothes?"

Rebecca looked sympathetic. "I'm sorry, miss. They were ruined. I disposed of them."

Miranda nodded. "Of course. I see." She sighed. "Well, then." She smiled at Rebecca. "I'll reimburse you for all of this. You might have to be a little patient with me, though. A little bit every week, like."

Rebecca laughed and waved Miranda's words aside. "Oh, miss, I haven't explained properly at all! I'm sorry. I thought you knew. Madam wishes to make you a gift of these items. There is no obligation in the case. Madam is grateful for your ... friendship ... with young Mister Shepard. We're all very grateful, miss. Myself, Hanson, Carlo, even Cook."

Miranda recalled the phone call Shepard had made to Pietro's brother. It could not be a coincidence. "Who is Carlo?" asked Miranda.

"Carlo is—was—madam's chauffeur, miss."

Miranda was alarmed. "Was?! Did something happen to Carlo?!" Surely the tragedy was not to be compounded further.

"Carlo left us this morning, miss. He had a death in the family, and he is returning home to Sicily. That is why Hanson is driving madam today."

Miranda began to put pieces together. "Did Carlo have a brother named Pietro?"

"Pietro was Mister Shepard's chauffeur, miss. Pietro and Carlo were twins." Rebecca's eyes filled with tears, and she produced a linen handkerchief from somewhere to dab at her nose. "I'm sure you know Pietro was killed in the same accident that injured Mister Shepard. We're all saddened, of course, but Carlo ... Carlo is devastated. And he dreads telling his mother. He feels he must be with her; he can not give her this news by telephone."

Tears burned behind Miranda's eyes. "Of course. I'm sorry for the loss of your friend. Pietro was a wonderful person, and he was much, much more than a chauffeur to Shepard."

"They were like brothers—the three of them," said Rebecca with a sniffle, "all through school together. And then they refused to be parted when Mister Shepard came back to the states. Fine boys. All three of them."

Miranda stepped close and opened her arms. Rebecca allowed herself to be enfolded in a hug, and together they wept.

At noon, when the nurses awakened Shepard to attempt a meal, he was muddle-headed and vague. He was aware of Miranda and of his mother, but he was not clear-minded enough to realize the relationship between the women had radically changed. Miranda helped by feeding him from his lunch tray. The effort of eating exhausted him, and he dozed off before cleaning his plate.

Miranda declared that she would stay at his bedside until he woke again. Neither Hermione nor any member of the hospital staff was brave enough to suggest Miranda should leave. Miranda Ogilvy, it seemed, was no longer invisible; she had become a force of nature – literally overnight.

Hermione Montgomery-Krausse retired to the VIP family suite, where she found Hanson conversing with two men in rumpled suits. The men flashed badges and introduced themselves as homicide detectives.

"Is this about the attempt on my son's life?" Hermione asked.

"No, ma'am," said the senior detective. "I'm afraid we have bad news."

23 THE DETECTIVES

Mrs. Montgomery-Krausse sat ramrod straight and, although obviously emotional, maintained the family dignity with undiminished fortitude. Hanson and Rebecca stood sentinel behind the sofa where she sat, and the two homicide detectives sat in two occasional chairs placed in front of her. One of the detectives jotted notes in a small leatherette-bound notebook as she spoke.

"He had told me he was going to expose a bid-fixing operation that had gone on for about a year," Hermione said. Her nose was red, her eyes swollen, but her voice was strong. "He was going to name the guilty parties both inside and outside the governor's office, even though it might cost him his reputation. His political enemies would, of course, pounce on any opportunity to make Reginald appear corrupt."

"Yes, ma'am," the senior detective said, glancing at the notes the other man was taking. "Did the governor ever tell you any of the names of these so-called 'guilty parties' he was going to expose?"

Hermione paused as if to search her memory. "I know one name, if I can remember it. There was a building contractor who held an ownership interest in several companies. His companies always seemed to know what the competing bids were, and they always came in just under the lowest bid. They always seemed to get the contracts. And they always seemed to bill the State for much more than they had quoted in their bid."

"Can you recall the name?" said the detective.

Hermione looked at the ceiling and seemed to think out loud. "What was it? Westinghouse ... Westwood ... Wechsler ... West ... Lake! Westlake! The man's name was Something Westlake! Is there a building contractor named Westlake?"

The detectives looked at one another. The one with the notebook paged back through his notes and referred to a scribbled page. "Bertram Westlake? Is that the name?"

"That's it!" Hermione said, and she smiled at the men. "But surely you don't think that man, that Westlake, could have killed the governor? This is a businessman, not a mobster. Perhaps it was simply a robbery. Reginald often carried large sums of cash, and he wore expensive watches and rings and such."

One man closed his notebook; both men stood. "It doesn't appear to have been a robbery, Mrs. Krausse. And a businessman with power and a motive can be as dangerous as a mobster. We'll certainly check it out."

First one and then the other man offered a parting handshake. Hermione sniffled daintily into a tissue provided by Rebecca. "Thank you for coming," Hermione said.

"Thank you for your time, ma'am. We're very sorry for your loss," said one detective.

"And please give Shep our best wishes for a speedy recovery," said the other. "We're big fans of Shep and Dave."

"Thank you. I'll tell him," said Shepard's mother.

Rebecca showed the men to the door of the suite. She asked for and received their business cards. After closing the door, Rebecca retrieved an iPad from a briefcase stowed beneath the coffee table. She added the detectives' contact information to the device.

All was silence in the suite until the resonating elevator bell indicated that the detectives had left the sixth floor. Then Hanson asked, "Are you all right, madam?"

Hermione's face hardened, her tears dried up, and her jaws clinched. "Westlake and Reggie were up to their beady eyeballs in corruption, but I was willing to look the other way until they tried to kill my son. I would happily shoot Reginald Montgomery myself if it were possible."

She turned to Rebecca as if she had been reminded of something. "Did you speak with Carlo?" Hermione asked.

"Yes, madam," Rebecca answered. She tapped the screen of her iPad and, after viewing the resulting screen, added, "The wire transfer has been posted to the Credit Lyonnais branch in Milan. The flowers will be delivered to Signora Fratelli late tomorrow, after Carlo arrives home."

Hermione nodded. "Hanson, has the other matter been attended to?"

"It is in the trunk of Mr. Westlake's personal vehicle," said Hanson.

"Excellent," said Hermione. "Rebecca, you have the disposable phone?"

"Yes, madam."

"Drive at least five miles away from the hospital—find a crowded mall parking lot, if you can—and place the call from there. Ten seconds, no more. Follow the script. Then dispose of the phone and return home. Take precautions so that you are not followed."

"Yes, madam." Rebecca snapped her briefcase shut and left the suite.

After a moment, Hermione turned toward Hanson. "You're certain those thugs were hired by Westlake?"

"My source is never wrong in such matters, madam. One of the men had set fire to Miss Ogilvy's house previously."

"There is no doubt both men are dead."

"None whatsoever, madam. Mr. Shepard dispatched one and a neighbor, a Mrs. Cleary, the other. The men were known criminals; they were armed. No charges will be filed against your son or his neighbor for protecting themselves."

"Excellent. The murder weapon will be traced to Phyllis Ogilvy, of course."

"Unfortunately, yes."

Hermione wrinkled her brow in concern. It was a new concern, and she was uncomfortable expressing it. "I, ah, we do not wish Miss Ogilvy to come under suspicion. She has fired the weapon before. There will be fingerprints."

Hanson smiled serenely. It was good to see madam softening toward the young lady whom Hanson had come to admire. "Have no fear, madam," he said. "First, there will be no fingerprints on the item. Second, Miss Ogilvy reported it stolen the night of the fire at her house. Third, at the time of the governor's death, Miss Ogilvy was in the Little Cypress Forest running for her life. A dozen police officers and emergency medical technicians can verify that. The young lady is above suspicion."

"And, I daresay, above reproach in your estimation," said Hermione with a knowing look.

"Indeed, madam," said Hanson with a nod that was nearly a bow.

"Perhaps I shall come to agree with you," Hermione mused, mostly to herself. She stood and gathered her handbag and gloves. "Take me home, please, Hanson. Shepard is in good hands here, and you and I need to rest and await Rebecca's return. I have a feeling the evening news will be fascinating tonight."

24 THE AWAKENING

Shepard Krausse recognized the smells first. Disinfectant, strong laundry detergent, stale institutional food, flowers, and the unmistakable, ineradicable underpinning aroma of urine. *Oh, yeah,* he thought. *Hospital.*

He felt the firm mattress, the institutional linens, the metal side rails of the bed. He felt the adhesive tape around the intravenous needle in his left arm, the tubing snaking across his left hand and taped again.

He heard nurses and visitors speaking softly in the hallway, shoes padding along the tile floor, metal carts with wheels rattling across the grout lines. He heard the hospital intercom paging doctors and calling codes.

He felt a dull ache in his head. Below his knees, the seared tissue on the backs of his legs demanded his attention. He forced that pain aside and concentrated instead on the sensation that intrigued him more than all the others. Something warm and heavy rested against his ribcage, and something soft enfolded his right arm and hand.

Carefully and slowly, he slid his arm and hand free of the surrounding warmth. He explored with his fingers a long, thick braid. He discovered a pair of eyeglasses pushed askew because the wearer's face was half buried in Shepard's torso. He smiled when he heard a delicate, ladylike snore.

Shepard had no idea how long he had been there. He remembered the Little Cypress, the helicopter, doctors and nurses waking him, poking him, talking at him through a fog. He thought his mother had been there, maybe more than once. Probably he had been out of things for a day or two.

He was sure of only a few things. His best friend, Pietro, was dead. His partner, friend, helper, and navigator, Dave, had died as well. And since the explosion that had plunged him into hell (or at least purgatory), the one constant in his life had been by his side.

No matter how groggy and unfocused he had been, he had never awakened without knowing she was there. He could not see her, of course. She didn't always speak, so he didn't always hear her. But he always smelled her or felt her or — and this was the crazy part —sometimes he just sensed her. It was as if some gravitational pull caused his heart to turn in her direction. When she was there, he knew it. He simply knew it.

He stroked her hair back from her temple, again and again, soothing himself with the warmth and texture of her. Soon he craved more. He wanted to hear her, talk to her, be conscious of her being conscious of him. He couldn't help himself. He had to wake her.

"Bean," he whispered.

No response. He stroked her hair once more, then gently tugged on the long braid.

"Bean," he said, a little louder. "Rise and shine, sweet Bean."

"They're not called sweet beans, they're called sweet *peas*," she answered without opening her eyes.

"Once a librarian, always a librarian," he said with a chuckle.

When he laughed, the movement of his diaphragm succeeded where his voice had failed: her head popped up and she blinked at him. She smiled and straightened her glasses on her face.

"You're awake!" she said.

"And finally that makes two of us," he said. "Where does it say I sleep on the bed and you sleep on me? Not that there's anything wrong with that. We can explore the concept in greater depth when I get out of here, if you like."

She laughed, took his hand from the end of her braid, and planted a kiss in his palm. "You really are awake; you're talking dirty."

"Sweet Bean, if you think that's 'talking dirty,' you need to get out more," he teased.

She wrapped his hand in both of hers and hugged it to her. She sobered, then asked, "Hurt?"

"Would you think me unmanly if I whimpered just a little?" he asked with a wry half-smile.

Miranda hit the call button before he even finished speaking. "We'll take care of that right now," she vowed.

"Patience," he soothed. "Hospitals are understaffed, nurses are super busy, they'll come when th—"

"Yes, Miss Ogilvy," interrupted a nurse, who seemed to have sprinted to the room.

"Mr. Krausse is awake and he's in pain," Miranda said imperiously. "He needs something right away, please."

"I'll be right back," said the nurse, and she disappeared.

Miranda relaxed against the bedside and kissed Shepard's hand again.

Shepard was mystified by the exchange between Miranda and the nurse. He was still agape when the nurse rushed again into the room. She injected something into Shepard's intravenous tube. "If that's not better in five minutes, just let me know," she said kindly. She smiled at Miranda and left.

He pulled free of Miranda's hands and placed his hand under her chin. He turned her face toward him and ran his fingers over her features. "Who is this person who has terrorized the nursing staff, and what have you done with Miranda Ogilvy?" he said.

"It just got to the point where there was too much at stake to sit back and be unseen," she said. "I was so afraid for you. I had to stand up and make people take notice. I had to make things happen; I couldn't wait for someone to 'get around to it.' You could've ... you really scared me."

He picked up her hand and brought it to his lips. "I'm sorry," he said, and kissed each finger in turn, saying "I'm sorry, I'm sorry, I'm sorry, I'm so sorry."

"Not your fault," she said. "Great apology, though. I think my toes just curled right up." She watched his eyes. They seemed to be only half open.

"How's the pain now?" she asked.

"Ooh, baby, we got to get a bottle of this stuff to take home," he said. "I can't even remember what was hurting. Great stuff."

"Shepard, don't go to sleep, okay? Stay with me a few more minutes," Miranda said, chafing his hand. "I need to tell you some things."

He forced his chin up and shoved more energy into his shoulders and arms. "Bad news," he said. "All right. I'm ready."

"I'm sorry to have to tell you, but your uncle, the governor, has been killed," Miranda said. She watched him for a reaction. There was nothing.

"They arrested a man named Westlake—a building contractor. The police said Westlake defrauded the State of millions, and the governor was getting ready to expose it, so Westlake killed him." She waited for Shepard's response.

"Westlake killed him," Shepard repeated softly. When he didn't say more, Miranda continued.

"Yeah, and then it gets really weird," Miranda said. "You remember when that guy set the fire in my house, and my shotgun went missing? And we reported it stolen, and the police assumed the arsonist took it. But I thought the arsonist wasn't carrying anything when he ran out, and I didn't think he had been in that part of the house even, but the only other person who had been in my house was your mother, and she didn't take my shotgun, I promise you, so I guess the police were right. Right?"

"I think I followed all that," Shepard said.

"The police think the arsonist was one of the guys who tried to kill us in the woods the other night. And they think those two guys were working for—get this now—"

"Westlake," he finished for her.

"Yeah," she said. "But that's not the weird part. Guess what they found in the trunk of Westlake's car?"

"Jimmy Hoffa? Or did they already find him somewhere else? I forget."

"My missing shotgun!" Miranda said. "And that's what Westlake used to murder the governor. Is that not totally weird?"

Shepard nodded, mulling over all the interlocking pieces of the unholy puzzle. Speaking more to himself than to Miranda, he said, "Iggy murdered Phyllis Ogilvy. Phyllis Ogilvy's twelve-gauge killed Reggie Montgomery. And Bertram Westlake is going to be convicted of the murder."

"We don't have proof that Iggy murdered Aunt Phyllis," said Miranda.

"I don't need proof," Shepard said. He thought a moment. "But if Uncle Reggie was 'Iggy,' then Phyllis got her justice."

"Oh gosh golly," breathed Miranda. "But how could the Westlake guy get Aunt Phyllis' shotgun? Even if Westlake hired my arsonist, I'm sure the arsonist didn't take that gun from my house. How did Westlake end up with the gun?"

Shepard thought. He shook his head, understanding. "Snake Day," he said.

"What?"

"Everybody in the family heard the story of the day you killed the rattlesnake. I told Pietro, Pietro would've told Carlo, Carlo would've told the household staff, and Hanson would definitely have told my mother."

Miranda shook her head. "But your mother came to my house after that, and she never mentioned it."

"And how did my mother get to your house?" Shepard asked.

"In her car."

"With her chauffeur. Carlo."

"Your mother's chauffeur took my shotgun?! Why?" Miranda was shocked.

"My controlling, overprotective, queen-of-the-world mother could not have me living next door to a lunatic who was liable to go blasting away at the slightest provocation. She couldn't move me, and she couldn't move you, so she removed the lunatic's weapon. Problem solved."

Miranda considered his logic and recalled everything she could about his mother's visit to her house. It was possible. It was feasible. It began to seem more and more probable.

"Carlo took the shotgun," Miranda agreed.

Shepard nodded. "Carlo, whose brother was murdered by Iggy and Iggy's partner—who appears to have been Bertram Westlake."

Miranda's eyes widened and she leaned closer to Shepard's ear to speak more quietly. "You think Carlo knew that Iggy was Governor Montgomery!"

"Servants always know everything," Shepard said. "Anyone who says differently has never had servants."

"But Carlo could be arrested for murder—and they have the death penalty in this state!"

"Castor Bean, Carlo will never be arrested for murder. He's long gone, back to his family in Sicily. Do you know anything about families in Sicily? They have a peculiar relationship with law enforcement—especially foreign law enforcement. Even if there were evidence against Carlo, he would never be turned over to American authorities."

Miranda nodded, taking it all in. "But there won't be any evidence against Carlo, will there."

Shepard smiled. "Very good, Grasshopper. The only evidence—the murder weapon—was undoubtedly planted very near poor Mr. Westlake. And the police undoubtedly received an anonymous tip from an untraceable phone, telling them exactly where to find said evidence."

They were quiet then. Each in their own way relived the horror of the explosion and the pursuit through the woods. There were no winners, but at least there were survivors.

Miranda leaned over and kissed Shepard's cheek. "Thank you for saving my life," she whispered.

"We saved each other," he replied. "We just couldn't save everyone."

After he fell asleep, Miranda gently wiped the tears from his cheeks and beard.

25 THE GIFT

The next morning, Miranda returned from the hospital cafeteria with coffee and cinnamon rolls for two. She turned into Shepard's room to find his mother standing at his bedside.

"Good morning, Mrs. Montgomery-Krausse," Miranda said. "We were just about to have coffee. Can I get you something?"

"Thank you, no. I've only come to bring you your car keys." Hermione lifted a key on its electronic key ring toward Miranda. "Since you arrived here with Shepard on the helicopter, you will need a way to get home."

Miranda put the coffee cups and sweet rolls down on the rolling bedside table and edged the table closer to Shepard. Shepard lifted a hand toward her and she took it, but she did not take the proffered keys.

"I appreciate the gesture. I hadn't even thought about how I would get home," said Miranda. "But I'm afraid those are not my keys." She turned to peel open the sipping slot on the coffee cups.

"Bean," said Shepard, grinning broadly. "Take the keys."

Miranda placed his coffee cup in his hand and arranged his sweet roll near him on the table that now overhung the bed. "Shep, they aren't mine. Mine are scratched and beat up and hanging from an Ernest Hemingway key chain. Cinnamon bun at your two o'clock, on the tray table."

Hermione nearly smiled. "You have Ernest Hemingway on a key chain?"

"Souvenir of a weekend in Key West," Miranda explained. "Librarian humor."

"Humor?" said Hermione, raising one eyebrow.

"I guess you had to be there."

"Indeed." Hermione turned away from the bed and crossed to the window. Looking down into the parking lot, she motioned for Miranda to join her. "Let me show you something, Miss Ogilvy, if you please."

Miranda looked toward Shepard. He sipped his coffee. When he didn't hear her move, he waved her in the direction of his mother's voice. "Go, go. She hasn't bitten anyone since we increased her medication weeks ago."

"Shepard, behave," said his mother. "Come here, Miss Ogilvy. Come, come."

Miranda walked around the foot of the bed and joined Hermione at the window. "Please, call me Miranda," she said.

Hermione nodded. "Yes, you must grow tired of Shepard referring to you as a vegetable. String Bean, is it?"

"It's Castor Bean," said Shepard. "Inside joke."

Hermione gave him a look but refused to dignify his statement with a response. She touched Miranda's elbow and pointed out the window.

"Do you see the blue Mercedes beside the valet parking kiosk?" said Hermione.

"It's beautiful. Is it new?" asked Miranda. "Oh, I see. You had to replace the one that was ... the one that burned."

"Yes, it is new," said Hermione, "and, no, it is not a replacement for Shepard's previous vehicle. This car is yours."

Shepard added, "Your old car is in the trunk."

Miranda looked from Hermione to Shepard to the blue Mercedes and back to Hermione. "You're serious!"

Before Hermione could answer, Shepard said, "It was ordered before the ... before the fire. Took this long to finally deliver it. Now take a deep breath and accept the keys."

"But—"

"Miranda, I'm being discharged today, and you are giving me a ride home. I refuse to ride in that sardine can you call an automobile! Take the keys!"

Miranda held out a hand, palm up, and Hermione deposited the keys on her palm. "Wow. If Shep's upset enough to call me 'Miranda,' I guess I have no choice." She wrapped Hermione in a bear hug that lasted almost long enough for Hermione to recover from the shock of such contact. "Thank you, thank you, thank you!" said Miranda.

"Thank *me*, why don'tcha? I'm the hero. Mother's just the messenger," Shepard said with a smile.

Miranda released Hermione. "Thank you, Shepard," Miranda said quietly.

"That's it?!" Shepard exclaimed. "That's all I get? Maybe you didn't get a good look at the car. It's the blue Mercedes. Look again. I think a gift like that deserves a more ... tangible ... thank you!"

"I saw it," Miranda said, and winked at Hermione. "It's very nice. I'll thank you again at home. Let's pack up your things and get you out of here."

"I'll deal with the business office downstairs while you get things in order here," said Hermione. "And, Shepard, there will be no 'tangible thanking' of people in this room. It's far too public. I expect behavior becoming a Montgomery." She left.

"Yes, mother," Shep drawled.

Miranda laughed and began collecting the toiletries and clothing articles that Rebecca and Hanson had been bringing to Shepard's room daily. She realized that she would have to pack up her own things from the VIP family suite, also. She probably had a lot of dead houseplants back in Minokee after many days away, but she had a slew of new clothes and a new car. Any minute now she expected to wake up.

Shepard was in the bathroom, easing carefully into loose-fitting shorts and a Ralph Lauren Polo shirt for the drive home. Miranda was closing his suitcase when Rebecca knocked on the doorjamb and entered with a small suitcase and overnight bag. The luggage was elegant. Miranda had never seen it before.

"I took the liberty of packing your things from the guest suite, miss," said Rebecca, setting the luggage down inside the door. "Hanson will be here momentarily to carry yours and Mister Shepard's things to your car."

Miranda took a deep breath. "Wow."

"We have had Mister Shepard's house and lawn cleaned, and the refrigerator and pantry are stocked with fresh groceries. The neighbors have worked out a schedule whereby someone will bring over a casserole every afternoon for the next seven days. Madam should have engaged a new chef and chauffeur for Mister Shepard by then."

"No, madam should not," Shepard interrupted, emerging from the bathroom. "Thank you for everything, Rebecca. You and Hanson have been more than helpful, and I appreciate your dedication and thoroughness."

"It is our pleasure entirely, sir," said Rebecca, blushing. Her schoolgirl reaction to the man's attention proved yet again to Miranda that Shepard "Adonis" Krausse affected women of all ages. "Shall I convey your wishes to madam as to the hiring of servants, then, sir?" asked Rebecca.

"I'll speak to her myself, thank you," said Shepard. "No need for you to face the wrath of the Medusa on my account." He smiled in her direction, and Rebecca's face glowed in response.

The next quarter-hour was eventful as Hanson came to take luggage to the car, Rebecca left to attend to secretarial duties, a discharge aide delivered the wheelchair required for Shepard's departure, and Hermione returned from the business office with appropriate discharge papers for the nursing station. Shepard requested a moment alone with his mother, so Miranda withdrew to the hallway and closed the door of his room.

Miranda walked down the corridor to a water fountain, and when she returned the nursing staff were all frozen in their tracks at the station nearest Shepard's room. All eyes were on the closed door. At Miranda's arrival, the nurses and aides averted their eyes and quickly busied themselves or took themselves off to attend to something down the hall. Standing outside the door, Miranda could hear the shouting that had attracted the employees' attention.

"*I* will, that's who!" shouted Shepard. "Give me a little credit! I can run my own life, for pity's sake!"

The voice of Shepard's mother was an indistinct murmur through the thick door. Either Hermione was farther away from the door, or Shepard was yelling much louder than she. Miranda suspected the latter.

"No! I need to be on my own! Alone!" he was shouting.

Hermione responded insistently.

"It isn't like that with Miranda," he vowed. "We're friends. We had a traumatic experience together. She's been there for me. She is not my nurse! She is not my servant! She is not moving in with me! I am not moving in with her!"

Hermione's intonation rose in a question.

"Mother, I'm an adult! I have a home and a job! I don't need a caretaker!"

His mother seemed to state an opinion with considerable conviction.

He, of course, disagreed. "No, I do not! I'll decide that for myself if and when the time comes!"

Miranda felt a chill begin in the center of her chest and spread throughout her body. Her mind emptied itself of warm emotions and sunny imaginings. She had been at his side for days, never thinking past the hospital door. He wanted her to drive him home; he had said so. But for him, it ended there. She saw them together; he saw himself alone. She thought they were soul mates; he said they were friends. She had assumed a relationship that he wasn't even considering. In fact, his own words were clear on the subject. He didn't want or need anyone. Certainly not an invisible librarian.

The hospital room door swung open, jolting Miranda out of her reverie. Shepard wheeled himself into the corridor. "Let's go," he snapped at Miranda. When his mother stepped into the open doorway, he said to her, "Don't worry about me. I'm fine. I'll call you."

No one said anything else. Miranda fell in behind Shepard's wheelchair and pushed it toward the elevator.

They had a drive of more than two hours from the hospital to Minokee. The new car was quiet and comfortable; the two passengers were quiet but not comfortable.

After the first half-hour, Miranda said only, "Hurting?"

He replied only, "I'm okay."

Another half-hour passed. Miranda said, "The car is lovely. It rides so smoothly. Thank you. Again."

"You're welcome. Again."

About ten minutes later, Shepard added, "I know you're not ... you don't like receiving gifts—no, don't say anything. I hear you drawing a big breath to contradict me, but just ... just listen for a minute. When you get home, you're going to notice some things."

"What things?"

"Listen, please."

"Sorry."

"A new kitchen and a new washer and dryer. Oh, and your killer clothesline is gone."

"What!?"

"Miranda—"

"I can't accept those things from you!"

"Miranda—"

"You can't go around giving people whole rooms and, and, and major appliances!"

"Yes, I can. And a few minor appliances, too. Your toaster was toast."

"But you can't do that—"

"Miranda!" He raised his voice to a level that shocked her into silence. "I have a lot of money. Phyllis was my friend, you are my friend, her house—your house—is a special place to me. I wanted to repair the damage to your kitchen. And I was afraid your clothesline would decapitate me one day. It made me happy to do these things for the house—and for you. And I won't miss the money. And there are no strings attached. I mean, you know, I don't expect you to do anything in return. Except say thank you – one time only, please—and then forget it. Okay?"

Miranda swallowed a huge lump in her throat. The lump settled behind her sternum and lodged there, aching. *Say thank you and forget it. That's what he wants,* she thought. *It doesn't mean anything. We're friends, nothing more. I want to be alone. I don't need a caretaker. I'll be okay. Don't worry about me.*

"Miranda? Okay?"

Miranda cleared her throat and forced a smile onto her lips, because she was convinced he would hear it in her voice. "Okay. Thank you."

"Okay. Now, let's forget it."

I'll try, she thought, with little hope of success. She would always remember every second she had spent with him, from the first glimpse of him jogging toward her out of a summer sunrise. She could stay away, as he said he wanted, but she couldn't forget.

For the next hour, Miranda's mind raced up and down alleys of possible futures. Growing old alone in Phyllis' house. Selling Phyllis' house and moving to Alaska. Changing her name and appearance and moving to Peru. Moving to Sicily and tracking down Carlo for old times' sake. Becoming a recluse and owning forty-one cats. Learning the violin so she could play sad melodies in the middle of the night, because she couldn't sleep, because she had nightmares about Viking funerals where cars burned instead of boats.

Miranda might have been both encouraged and dismayed if she had known what phantoms and dreams swept through Shepard's mind during that same silent hour.

Shepard clinched his stomach muscles against the pain at the top of his diaphragm. His throat ached and his eyes burned. His hand twitched, fighting a compulsion to reach out and hold Miranda's small hand. For days now he had maintained a strong facade. The occasional tear had escaped, barely noticed, but he had not permitted himself to collapse in a flood of grief. Miranda's strength had become his when she held his hand or when he felt her at his side. But he knew his time was running out. His self-control was unraveling and would soon fall away like a broken string of beads. Then the pain would overtake him, and he was afraid he would start screaming and never stop.

The wall of denial he had built between himself and a future without Dave or Pietro was crumbling like ancient mud bricks. His imagination had been buried, but it was struggling to the surface. Soon it would force him to envision complete solitude — days and nights and weeks and months and years of it. No one to select his clothes, trim his beard, prepare his meals, collect his laundry, produce his program. Worse, no one to laugh with him and at him. No one to nag him to do better, to try harder, to take care, to get over himself.

How would he stay sane if he began to imagine running with no furry companion-and-guide? Sleeping with no warm, fuzzy beast beside the bed to guard, protect, and amuse him? Showering with no bubble-covered bear shape sharing the spray? Having no 24/7 shadow to read his thoughts, send him signals, telepathically give advice, accept blame for any foolishness?

Shepard had fought to stave off the emotional pain, refused to admit the loss, declined to experience the grief, but he was reaching the end of his strength. Soon he would lose it completely, go (at least temporarily) insane, and weep for days or weeks. He wanted no witnesses to that fiasco when it happened. He needed to get home as fast as possible, lock himself in, and lock everyone else out.

When Miranda pulled the car to a stop in Shepard's driveway, she broke the hour-long silence with an unnecessary, "We're here."

Shepard swung open the passenger door. The smells of earth and plants hovered in the humid breeze. The susurrations of shifting leaves and mosses whispered high above. Delicate melodies of mockingbirds floated down from the trees. He was home in Minokee, his heart had fractured, and he could feel the pieces spreading farther and farther apart. He had to hurry and hide himself away before the crashing began.

Miranda retrieved his suitcase from the trunk and carried it to his door. Even slowed by his injured legs and forced to walk with a cane, he was already crossing the threshold when she reached the doorstep. She leaned in far enough to set his bag in the foyer. He seemed distracted, his face turned away from her. She had been preparing herself for this moment.

"I know you need some alone time," she began, hoping that miraculously he would contradict her and ask her to stay.

He didn't.

"I hate to leave you," she said. It was only the truth. "Just promise me one thing."

"What?" he said without turning. His voice was low and hoarse.

"Promise me you won't do anything dangerous? You won't do anything that could, you know, harm you?"

"No, of course not," he said, nodding. "Thanks for everything. I'll call you."

He turned only enough to shut the door quickly.

Miranda turned and ran to the car.

By the time she had the motor started, her vision was blurred by tears and her body jerked with sobs. Carefully she backed out of Shepard's driveway, praying she could drive around the block to her own house without hitting anything.

Had she remained on the doorstep two seconds longer, Miranda would have heard the desperate keening of a lost soul. Shepard had indeed abandoned all sanity and vented his pain in uncontrolled weeping, yelling, moaning, and pounding of fists.

He stumbled to his room and fell face down across the bed. There he remained, crying piteously, until, at least an hour later, the physical agony of his burns forced him to get up and seek his pain medication.

26 THE FACTS

Miranda was grateful for the opportunity to return to work at the library the following Monday. She was unable to sleep at night and unable to find enough diversions for her mind during the day, if she remained at home.

The commute was certainly more pleasant in her new car than it would have been in her tin-can toy car, but parking was more of a challenge. She coped by positioning her baby blue behemoth at the farthest corner of the library parking lot, where there was nothing for her to hit—or to hit her. Of course, she would have to walk a half-marathon from her car to the library door, but that was no problem. Miranda always wore sensible shoes.

Annabelle had maintained the status quo in Miranda's absence. The result was a week's worth of returned books still piled on piles of piles, waiting to be shelved. After all, there was no question that Annabelle's delicate manicure took precedence over mere service to the reading public.

Since Miranda arrived early, even after walking ten minutes from her car, no one was there to see the smile with which she piloted the first of many overstuffed book carts out into the stacks.

As early morning gave way to mid-morning, Annabelle made her entrance and took up her throne at the checkout counter. There she would reign over her literary serfs as they brought their check-in offerings to her like taxes to the manor's lord. There she would dispense checked-out volumes like a regent dispensing boons to the peasantry. Most of all, throughout the day, she would bewitch all mere men with her sultry beauty, like Morgan Le Fey.

With so much to do, it was no wonder Annabelle had little time to devote to other aspects of the library: books, shelves, fellow employees. So it was that when Miranda returned to the counter to deliver an empty cart and pick up another load of books for shelving, Annabelle was oblivious.

"Hi!" bubbled Miranda. "How've you been?"

Annabelle seemed confused and spent a second seeking the source of the voice chirping at her. Her eyes settled on Miranda at last. "Hello, Marianne. How're you?" Annabelle looked away again.

"Well," Miranda chimed, "not sure if I'm good or bad, but at least I'm back." She chuckled at her feeble, attempted humor.

"Back from where?" said Annabelle.

Some things never change, thought Miranda, but she said, "Doesn't matter," and rolled her book-laden cart out of Annabelle's sight and definitely out of mind.

. . . .

At one 'clock that Monday, when Miranda was eating her tuna salad and reading *Finding Your Own Way to Grieve* in the park near the library, people were stirring in far-off Minokee.

Martha Cleary trundled up the front steps of the Krausse house carrying in a basket her famous broccoli-chicken-cheddar casserole, steaming beneath a thick towel. She balanced the warm bundle on one forearm and knocked loudly on the front door with the opposite fist.

She waited.

She knocked again, louder.

More waiting.

She pounded hard enough to rattle the glass in the living room windows.

"Who is it!?" snapped an unfriendly baritone some distance from the other side of the door.

"It's your neighbor with your dinner, boy! Open up!" shouted Martha.

"I'm comin', I'm comin'. Hold your horses," the same grumpy voice responded.

Moments later the door opened. Martha shoved her way past Shepard, who maneuvered his cane to keep his balance as she barreled through. He shut the door and turned toward the kitchen. Martha had gone straight to his refrigerator with the confidence of a long-time family friend. She plucked an empty jelly jar out of the refrigerator door and tossed it into the trashcan across the room. Then she rearranged the contents of the refrigerator shelves so she could insert her casserole.

"It's right out of the oven, but I can see you ain't ready to do justice to a decent meal at the moment, so I'm putting it away. You kin put some on a plate an' nuke it when you want it." Martha shut the fridge and turned to look at the man waiting in the doorway, leaning heavily on his cane. "Dang, ya look like the very devil," she said.

"Thanks for the food, Miz Martha," he said with more etiquette than enthusiasm. "Smells really good."

"Course it does," she said. "Consider the source!"

"Yes, ma'am," he said politely.

"Look at yerself!" Martha ordered.

"Ma'am?" he said.

"I know ya've had a hard time, and I'm truly sorry fer yer loss and all. But, dang it, boy, if yer Grandma and Grandpa Krausse could see you now, they'd have a hissy fit! There's no excuse fer lettin' yerself go like this! It ain't healthy! Boy, I can see I need to take you in hand, fer yer Grandma's sake if fer nothin' else."

Shepard backed away and tottered into the living room as if to show his visitor to the door. "I'm fine, Miz Martha, really," he said. "Nurse comes by once a day, physical therapist comes four times a week. Got plenty of pills. Thanks again for the food." He actually reached for the doorknob, but he was overly optimistic.

"Jest git away from the door, I ain't leavin' 'til I'm good and ready," Martha asserted. "Now sit yerself down here. There's things gotta be said." She sat on one end of the couch and slapped the middle couch cushion a resounding whack.

Shepard Krausse had known Martha Cleary all his life. Even though he was tired, in pain, and incapable of complex contemplation or elegant articulation, he was lucid enough to know when there was no alternative but surrender. He hobbled to the couch and sat, easing his burned legs into a nearly comfortable position.

"You say you're doin' okay?" asked Martha.

"I get the feeling you're about to disagree," Shepard said with a sigh.

"Yer durn tootin'!" she said. "Look at ya! Yer hair looks like raccoons been nestin' in it. Ya got food and some kinda pink or red liquid spilled in yer beard. Yer shoes don't match. Yer shirt don't go with them shorts—lord, ain't no shirt ever been made that'd go with them shorts, they's hideous. Yer shirt ain't buttoned right, neither. Yer eyes is sunk like ya ain't slept since Lincoln was president. Yer pants is hanging on ya all scarecrow-like, so I know you ain't been eatin'—prolly since it happened. By the way, you ain't smellin' like no rose, neither."

She stopped and seemed to await his reaction.

"Yeah. So?" he said.

"Tell me the truth, Speedy: are you capable of taking care of yourself or not?" asked Martha.

"I am capable of taking care of myself, Miz Martha," Shepard said.

"Then why ain't ya doin' it?" she snapped. "Yer not feeling well, yer hurtin', yer sad, life stinks right now. I get that! You lost two good friends. Sure. But you ain't lost yer *last* friend. You got people around ya wantin' to help ya. Ya got a little gal right next door who'd do anything for ya. And you ain't even doin' anything fer yerself!"

"People wouldn't want to be so nice to me if they knew what really happened."

Martha swallowed the first words that came to her mind. She took a calming breath and said, "I find that hard to believe. Just what do you think 'really happened'?"

"The whole thing was my fault, and I walked away scot-free."

"Beg to differ on that, but go on with the story."

Shepard sighed and slumped back into the cushions. "Pietro told me to stop, but I just kept talking it up, on the air, night after night, thinking the Great Shepard Krausse was bullet-proof. Man, I was such an arrogant S.O.B. I know the Montgomery clan, and I know what kind of self-important, amoral stuffed shirts they run around with. If anybody knew what they were capable of, it should've been me. Instead, I chose to live in my fantasy world where the bad people fear the law, and the guilty get punished, and the innocent go to Disney World. Stupid me. I poked at the monsters until they fought back. Then I was surprised that they fought dirty."

Martha patted his knee with one knobby-veined hand. She waited, and after a moment he went on.

"We were leaving for work," he said. "Pietro was behind the wheel, I had just let Dave into the back seat, and I said I had to go back in the house and get my cellphone. Pietro said he'd get it, but I said no, I was halfway there already. Dave started to get out of the car and come with me, but I told him to stay."

His voice broke when he said, "He stayed. They both stayed in the car."

He stopped to breathe deeply and collect himself.

Martha said, "And we all know what happened next."

"Oh, no, Miz Cleary, you don't know the best part – the really stupid part: Bean found my cellphone after the explosion. It was in my friggin' pocket the whole time. So not only did I provoke the monster, I staked my friends out for the slaughter like a goat tethered to a tree by tiger hunters. And I didn't even have the decency to die with them, because I was too dimwitted to know what was in my own pockets."

Martha said, "Shepard, honey, don't do this to yourself."

Shepard forsook good manners and shouted at the elderly lady, "Exactly what do you want me to do!? Huh? What will make everything all better?! Nothing! There's nothing for me to do! Nothing I could do will ever change what happened!"

"That's right, you cain't change what happened!" Martha shouted back at him. Then she stood, laid a comforting hand on his shoulder and said quietly, "But you can decide what happens next."

Shepard covered his eyes with one hand and dropped his chin to his chest.

Martha massaged his shoulder. "Now, I'm gonna do jest what yer Grandma Krausse would do if she wuz here. You take a shower, and I'm gonna help you organize your clothes and get spiffed up, then yer gonna eat a good home-cooked meal, and then yer goin' to git in bed and git some rest. Okay?"

He nodded.

Martha placed her hands under his arms and helped him stand. As they moved toward the bed- and bath-rooms, she scolded him, "An' the next time you answer a door, young man, you better be dressed and in yer right mind or I'll know the reason why. Get me?"

"Yes, ma'am," he said. Then after a second he added, "Thanks, Miz Cleary."

"Yer very welcome, Speedy Boy," she said.

27 THE LIST

Miranda trudged through the workweek, keeping busy at the library, going in early, staying late, reading during her breaks. The problem was the in-between time. While driving, cooking dinner, doing laundry, taking a shower, trying to sleep, she was having tremendous difficulty controlling her thoughts.

She spent a reasonable amount of time mourning and remembering Dave and Pietro, and that was okay. It was healthy to transition through all the stages of grief, about which she had been reading. She knew the pain of that loss would lessen over time, even though she would never forget them.

What was not healthy was her preoccupation with the one thing that was forbidden her. She recalled the prayer her mother had taught her: "Lord, give me the serenity to accept the things I cannot change, the courage to change the things I can, and the wisdom to know the difference."

Miranda wanted to be with Shepard Krausse.

He didn't want that.

It was something she could not change, and she was not serene about it.

If the situation was truly unchangeable, she wanted to accept that fact, wrap herself in serenity, and move on. She had prayed. She had tried to tell herself to simply accept. She had filled every minute of the day that she could fill. But every time she stopped praying, accepting, filling for even a minute, Shepard crowded into her mind.

Fourteen days had crawled by since Miranda had left Shepard at the door of his house and had run away. She had not seen him, spoken to him, or even spoken about him since the moment that door had closed between them.

She had given it her best efforts, but her serenity prayers just weren't working. She decided to look at the rest of the prayer. What about "the courage to change the things I can"? What about "the wisdom to know the difference"? What "difference"? The difference between "things I cannot change" and "things I can."

Miranda experienced an epiphany. She had made a mistake. She had placed her situation in the wrong category. It wasn't a "cannot-change" situation at all. It was definitely a "change-the-things-I-can" situation.

She finally knew the difference. Change was possible. Courage was the prerequisite. She had courage. She had shown it in dealing with police officers, emergency medical technicians, doctors and nurses, even Shepard's mother. Courage was a natural outgrowth of loving something or someone more than yourself. She knew she had that. Because she knew she loved Shepard Krausse.

Miranda resolved to take decisive action. She would charge the enemy lines; she would storm the battlements; she would fearlessly face the foe. She would make a list.

Several hours later, Miranda was putting the finishing touches on her hair and—yes—her makeup. It was only blusher and lip gloss, but it was more than Miranda usually wore. The irony was not lost on her, of course, but she primped to make herself feel attractive. It didn't matter that no one was going to actually see her. Satisfied that she looked, and smelled, her very best, Miranda picked up the carefully typed list (on carefully chosen pale blue paper with high rag content), and exited her back door.

She tromped across her back yard, wondering if sandals had been the best choice for navigating wet grass. She passed through the break in the hedge and proceeded to the Krausse kitchen door. Holding the precious list in one hand, she knocked with the other.

"Coming," called the man of her dreams from somewhere inside the house.

Miranda's heart rate climbed. She switched the list from one hand to the other.

To Miranda's lonely eyes, the opening of that kitchen door was like a sunrise after three months of darkness. She drank in the sight of white-blond hair and beard, broad shoulders, blue eyes. "Oh, gosh golly, you look wonderful!" she exhaled without thinking.

The man's lips parted in a wide smile. "Castor Bean!" he said.

Miranda shoved the list into his hand, crumpling it in the process. "Here!"

He manipulated the paper between his fingers then used both hands to smooth the crinkles out of it. He held it up, "What is it?"

"It's a list," she said. "There are things we can't change and things we can change, and this list is to change some things we can change, and I know I have the courage to change these things and I'm pretty sure you have the courage to do it, too, but we'll never know if we don't, you know, talk it through. Step one. Talk it through. The list, I mean."

"Lord, I've missed you," said Shepard with a chuckle. "Come on in. I'll fix us some lemonade and you can tell me about step one and the list." He handed the paper back to her. "Would you mind holding this for me for a minute?"

"Oh, sure," she took the paper and followed him into the kitchen.

He still used his cane, but he was walking with less discomfort and more assurance. He had made excellent progress during the weeks since they had parted. She told him so while he put ice in glasses and poured from a pitcher of lemonade.

He offered her cookies a neighbor had baked for him, but she declined. Butterflies in the tummy, she said.

At last they sat opposite one another at the kitchen table.

"I think I have to take some things off the list already," Miranda said.

"Well, why don't you tell me what the list is, and we'll take it from there."

He sipped his lemonade and waited for her to explain.

Miranda thought for a moment about how best to begin.

"Here's the thing," she said finally. "I want to be with you, but you want to be alone. I think if we're objective and analytical about this situation, the situation can be changed."

"Bean, I—" he began.

"Wait!" she interrupted. "Let's just go down the list. Then if you still don't want me around, ... well, ... we'll cross that bridge if we come to it."

"But, Bean, I never—" he tried again.

"Item one," she spoke over him. "You're rich. You might think I'm after your money. But I'm not. You should know that I live rent-free, and I don't have a car payment—that's thanks to you now, but I didn't have a car payment before."

"You didn't have a real car before," he injected.

"I don't carry credit card debt, I give my tithe to the church, I have a retirement account with state civil service, I don't have any outstanding student loans, I don't have any addictions—not even to shopping—and I can still wear the clothes I wore in high school and college."

"Really," he said, sounding amused. "So, not a fashionista."

"Right," she said. "And that's not just good financially, because I don't spend a lot on clothes, it's also good relationally."

"It's good 'relationally' for you to wear old clothes?"

He covered his smile with one hand and held his lemonade with the other.

Miranda was ignoring her lemonade in her passion for her subject.

"It's perfect if I'm in a relationship with you, because you never see what I'm wearing! Isn't that great?"

He coughed behind his hand. "Great!"

"Plus, you probably have lawyers who can put together an ironclad pre-nup so I can never touch your money, anyway, right?"

"Right."

"So item one is off the list. You being rich has nothing to do with us being together."

"What a relief," he said.

"Yeah," she said, ignoring his sarcastic tone. "So we just strike that off the list. Have you got a pencil? I didn't bring a pencil, sorry."

"No prob," he said. "Drawer next to the pantry."

Miranda got up, went to the drawer, and brought back a pencil. She crossed off the first item with a flourish.

"What's number two?" asked Shepard, getting up to refill his lemonade glass. Miranda's was nearly untouched, and her ice was melting.

"Number two," said Miranda. "You're famous."

"I wouldn't say—"

"No. No, you're a local celebrity, you can't deny it. You have your own radio show."

"Actually, I may not go back to Sheep Counters," he said.

Miranda looked stricken. "What?" she said. "They can't fire you because of what happened. None of it was your fault. And you've been in the hospital and—"

"It's okay, Bean," Shepard said. "It may be time for someone else to host Sheep Counters. I'll still have a job. I won't fire me."

Miranda's brows furrowed. "You are your boss?"

"Sure," said Shepard. "I thought you knew that. It's no secret."

"You own the radio station?" Miranda asked, wide-eyed.

"I own five FM stations in four states," he said. "Is that a problem?"

Miranda thought about it. "No," she announced. "Owning a bunch of radio stations falls under item one— you're rich—and we already took care of item one, so no problem."

Shepard emitted a theatrical sigh of relief. "Thank goodness," he said.

"Anyway, about item two," Miranda continued. "You're famous and I'm nobody—"

"I object!" he slapped the table for emphasis. "I object to characterizing you as a nobody."

Miranda looked at him wryly. "No objections allowed. Don't get all lawyery on me or we'll never get through the whole list."

"Heaven forbid," he quipped.

"Anyway," Miranda went on, "even if we stipulate—how's that for lawyery—we stipulate that you're famous and I'm nobody, that would mean that you're famous and I'm not famous. But this is not a problem—"

"Agreed!" shouted Shepard.

"I'm not finished," said Miranda. "It's true that I am not famous. That doesn't mean I'm not important. I'm important to my family; I'm important to the people I help every day; I'm import—"

"To me," Shepard said. "You're important to me. And since you and I are the only people who count with regard to this list, item two is a wash. Next?"

"Right," said Miranda, crossing off item two with a sweep of her arm. "Item three: you're drop dead gorgeous and I'm as ugly as ten miles of bad road."

"What!?" Shepard yelled. "Are you crazy!?"

"Are you blind!?" she shouted. "Okay, that didn't come out right, but are you serious!? You don't have any idea how women—and a few men, okay—drool all over themselves when you walk by."

"Even if that were true, what does that have to do with you and me?" he asked.

"Shepard," she spoke as if explaining to a small child, "you don't want people to look at you and say, 'Why is that handsome guy hanging around with that skanky woman?' do you?"

"Skanky? You think you're skanky?" Shepard was incredulous. "What does that even mean? And who are these people? Obviously not anybody who knows you, because anyone who knows you knows you are the most beautiful person who's ever entered a library. And that's any library, anywhere."

"Oh, Shepard," she said softly. "That's sweet. But the truth is, I'm not pageant material. There's a line in *Jane Eyre* where Jane describes herself as 'poor, obscure, plain, and little,' and that's me exactly."

"Miranda Castor Bean Ogilvy, you listen to me," Shepard said, reaching out and finding her hand. He squeezed her fingers and said, "You are the most beautiful creature I have never seen. I veto item three. It's off the list." He let go of her hand. "Next!"

Miranda stared at him for five seconds, then ten.

"Bean?"

She shook her head in wonder at him then applied the pencil to item three. Gone.

"Item four," said Miranda. "Well, this one is probably no good any more."

"Why do you say that?"

"Okay, item four is a reason that we *should* be together."

"Sounds good, what is it?"

"You need someone to take care of you," said Miranda. "I know you told your mother that you don't need anyone, but I thought if you really gave me a chance, there would be things I could do for you."

"Bean—" he tried to interrupt, but she wouldn't hear him.

"When you opened the door a while ago, and I saw how perfect you look, how well your house is organized, and your kitchen—you probably cook better than I do—it's just," she began to cry, "if you could just be a tiny bit helpless, y'know? While you're recovering at least. Instead, you're all Chuck Norris against the bad guys in the woods, and then you're all Martha Stewart around the house, and—"

"Bean!" he stopped her. Again he took her hand, and this time he wrapped it in both of his. "Bean, Bean, Bean," he said soothingly. "You've got it all backward. It's not me who has been the hero in this relationship, sweetheart, it's you. All those days in the hospital when I wanted to fall apart, you were there, keeping me together. In the woods, if you hadn't been with me, I couldn't have taken on those thugs. You were my reason to keep going. On rainy mornings when I didn't want to go for a run, I went because I knew you would be waiting for me."

Miranda wiped her nose on the sleeve of her free arm. "But you told your mother you didn't want me around. You closed the door in my face and told me to go away and stay away."

Shepard rose from his chair, came around the table, and pulled Miranda up and into his arms. He hugged her to him and kissed the top of her head.

Laying his cheek against her hair, he told her, "I was a coward. I was afraid of looking weak in front of my overbearing mother, and that's understandable. But I was wrong to be afraid of letting you see me at my worst. I didn't want you to see me needing help."

Miranda wrapped her arms around his ribcage and held him tightly.

"You misunderstood what I said to my mother – which, I might add, is what you get for eavesdropping, Miss Big Ears. I don't want you to be my nurse, or my caretaker, or my cook, or my driver, my therapist, my butcher-baker-candlestick-maker. Bean, there's only one job opening for you, and I've told you a hundred times exactly what it is."

She could feel his tears falling into her hair. Gradually, her own tears ceased. Soon, she felt him pull himself together as well.

"What else is on that stupid list?" he said with a sniff and a chuckle.

"I forget," she answered.

He laughed.

"Shepard?" she began.

"Yes?"

"You used to propose to me every day."

"You used to say no every day," he reminded her. "No one would blame me if I got discouraged."

"Do you think you'll ever propose to me again?"

"Well, I have recently been told that I'm a courageous person. I might be strong enough to try again. You'll have to cut me some slack, though. It's kinda hard for me to get down on one knee right now. Probably be better in a few weeks. If I do manage to propose one last time, do you think you'll say yes for a change?"

"Depends. Would I have to be hyphenated?"

"You could be Castor hyphen Bean," he suggested with a smile.

"Deal," she said. "I think you should kiss me to seal the bargain."

He agreed.

THE END

MESSAGE FROM THE AUTHOR

Thank you for reading FINDING MIRANDA. I hope you have enjoyed reading it as much as I enjoyed bringing it to you.

Please share the book with others by giving it a good (but honest!) review at Amazon.com or Goodreads.com and by telling friends about it. Contact me at the addresses given on the succeeding page; I enjoy hearing your thoughts, questions, and suggestions. We're readers, you and I, and it's good for us to celebrate and encourage one another.

Happy reading.

Iris Chacon

CONNECT WITH IRIS CHACON

on

FACEBOOK/AUTHORIRISCHACON
TWITTER/@IRISCHACON1371
LINKEDIN/IRISCHACON
GOODREADS.COM
AMAZON.COM
SMASHWORDS.COM
CHRISTIANWRITERS.ORG
AND
HTTPS://WWW.AUTHORIRISCHACON.WORDPRESS.
COM

Send email to Iris Chacon by sending to:
[First name][Last name]137 at gmail dot com

Cover Art is by FIONA JAYDE at
http://fionajaydemedia.com

ABOUT THE AUTHOR

Native Floridians are comparatively rare. Iris Chacon's family first arrived in Florida when it was a Spanish colony, in the 1700s. In Iris's stories, her characters find romance, mystery, and joy on the peninsula and its islands. Iris is the mother of two. She and her husband have a small-town home in rural Florida, where her family members have lived since the early 1900s. In addition to ebooks and novels, Iris has written for radio, stage, and screen. She has worn many hats – including musician, teacher, and librarian.

SAMPLE CHAPTERS
FROM OTHER NOVELS BY
IRIS CHACON

SYLVIE'S COWBOY

SCHIFFLEBEIN'S FOLLY

MUDSILLS and MOONCUSSERS

DUBY'S DOCTOR

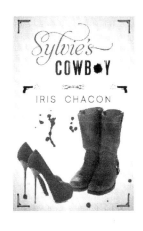

SYLVIE'S COWBOY

Sparks fly – often literally – when a Penthouse Princess is forced to move to the rustic ranch of a Crabby Cowboy. They clash in every way over everything, sometimes hilariously.

It would be funnier, however, if they weren't in danger from unknown murderous thieves.

Will they live long enough to learn to live together?

CHAPTER ONE – THE RANCH

Rural Florida, Outside Clewiston
Two Days Before the Explosion

A dove gray Mercedes Benz limousine bumped along a winding, rutted dirt road through palmetto bushes, spindly pines, and scrub oaks to stop at an open gate with a rusty cattle gap. On a plank above the gate someone had burned "McGurk Ranch" in simple block letters.

Harry Pace, lean, tanned, and dark-haired with silvering temples, slid out of the limo's back seat. He gestured to the driver to stay put, and walked over the cattle gap, through the gate.

Harry had walked farther than any sane person wanted to in the sticky Florida heat when at last he soundlessly approached the front door of the ranch's modest house. He gripped the doorknob. It was locked. He sidled to his left and peered in a window. Nobody inside. From behind the house, he heard someone whistling "Your Cheatin' Heart." Harry smiled to himself and moved in the direction of the music.

In the second-story loft of a hay barn, Walter McGurk was forking hay out the open hay door, sailing it into a battered red pickup truck parked below. The truck's doors were inexplicably yellow. Walt whistled as he worked.

Walt made a heavy job look easy with his strong, athletic build. Sweaty shirt sleeves rolled up to his elbows revealed ropes of muscle undulating in his sun-darkened forearms as he lifted and tossed the hay. His jeans were tight and faded from many washings. His tooled leather belt held a large hunting knife in a weathered cowhide sheath. He wore battered, scuffed cowboy boots.

Harry approached the barn, shielding himself from view beneath a huge avocado tree. When he eased around the tree, a big, ugly dog growled from beneath the red-and-yellow pickup. In the loft overhead, Walt jerked toward the sound and spotted Harry instantly.

"What do you want?" Walt growled, echoing the dog.

"What does any man want when his partners are stealing him blind?" asked Harry, stepping out from beneath the avocado shade.

Walt spun and hurled his pitchfork like a javelin. It thwacked into the ground a hair's breadth from Harry's boots. Only Harry's eyes moved.

"You ain't stupid enough to be talkin' about me," said Walt. "I ain't a thief. Fact, I'm the only half of *this* partnership that ever does an honest day's work. So, what do you want?"

Walt used the hayloft's rope and pulley to swing Tarzan-like to the ground. He paced to the truck, drying his face and wiping perspiration out of his hat with a bandana from his pocket. Walt opened the truck's passenger door and helped himself to water from an Igloo cooler.

Harry walked around the grounded pitchfork to join Walt at the truck. Walt filled a paper cup with water from the Igloo, but when Harry reached for it, Walt offered it instead to the ill-tempered dog lying under the truck. Unperturbed, Harry got his own cup of water. Then he turned his back on Walt and toyed with a heavy avocado drooping from a branch.

"Spit it out, will ya?" said Walt, helping himself to water from the paper cup he had shared with the dog. "Butch and me got things to do."

Harry didn't turn around. "I was gonna ask you to help me when I make my play to get back what they stole," Harry said to the avocado. "But it occurs to me you're probably gettin' too old and too slow."

Behind Harry, Walt bent to reach beneath his jeans and pull a pistol out of an ankle holster.

"I'm twenty years younger than you, old timer, and I can still chop my own guacamole," said Walt.

Harry snapped the avocado from the tree. The branch recoiled, bucking and swinging. Harry feinted one way, then reversed direction, turned, and threw the avocado high. It soared like a miniature green football far over Walt's head.

Walt fired three quick shots, each one chopping a piece off the airborne avocado.

Avocado chunks rained down and littered the grass. Harry walked through them, turning them over with the toe of his boot. Walt slid the pistol back into his own boot. Harry gave him a satisfied nod.

"I want you to take care of Sylvie," Harry said.

Walt shook his head. "I ain't up to spoiling your daughter for ya. You done too well already on that, if ya ask me."

Harry gave him a hard look. "Don't spoil her," he said. "Take care of her."

"You take care of her. Ain't seen her in nearly ten years. You and I both know she'd be happy if she never saw me again."

"I'll be busy," said Harry. "Gonna give some big city thieves a dose of their own medicine."

"And if they don't want to swallow it?"

Harry turned to leave, speaking almost to himself as he retraced the route to the limo. "Then we'll find out whether *I'm* gettin' too old and too slow."

Butch rose from beneath the truck, and Walt absently rubbed the dog's ears as he watched Harry go. Walt's brow furrowed, and there was both anger and worry in his voice when he shouted, "I got a good life here, Harry. Don't you mess it up for me, y'hear?! Harry?! I mean it, now."

Harry kept walking. He never looked back.

"Shoot!" said Walt in disgust. He splattered a hunk of avocado with a kick and snatched up the pitchfork to return to work. Harry was gone. Whatever would happen, would happen.

A cellular phone rang inside the truck. Walt walked over, leaned in, and plucked the phone from its holster on the dashboard.

"McGurk," he said into the phone. He listened, then responded, "Was that tonight? ... No, no problem. I just forgot is all. ... Clarice, people forget. It don't mean they don't love people. They just forget. I'll pick you up at seven. ... Fine. 'Bye."

He slammed the phone back into its holster and gave Butch an exasperated look. "I think what we need is one more fancy-planning, crazy-talkin', lipstick-wearin' tower of estrogen in our lives right now, don't you?"

"Woof!" said Butch.

CHAPTER TWO – THE OFFICE

Downtown Miami
One Day Before the Explosion

Leslye Larrimore was a 50-ish, elegantly coiffed woman who sported designer business attire and balanced effortlessly on five-inch stiletto heels. Leslye's office at Pace-Larrimore, Incorporated, was an expansive, opulent room with a stunning city view. Mahogany and brass shone everywhere around her as she read her mail at a desk the size of an aircraft carrier.

Harry Pace entered without knocking and sprawled in one of the elegant, upholstered guest chairs across from the desk. Leslye set her mail aside.

"Missed you at Sylvie's last Saturday," she said.

"I doubt if my daughter would agree with you," said Harry. "Surely Dan Stern was there to fill the void."

"Jealous? Harry, really."

"I'm not jealous, Les. I'm her father."

"And he's your business partner," said Leslye. "I should think you'd be pleased that they like each other. She's not daddy's little girl any longer, Harry. She's going to have other men in her life."

"Fine. Let her have *other* men. Les, can't you get Stern to lay off?"

"You want him to lay off, you tell him. Why are you so against Danny all of a sudden?"

Harry pursed his lips and clinched his fists. He bounced one fist on his knee. "He'll get his tail in a crack someday and do something desperate to get himself out of it. Heck, he may have done it already. I don't want Sylvie to be caught in a crossfire."

Leslye smiled and used her most soothing tones. "I really think you're overreacting," she said. "I don't see any of that happening. Really I don't."

Harry pushed himself up from the chair like a much older man. "I'll pass on dinner tonight, Les, if you don't mind," he told her. "Think I'll go out to the boat and spend the weekend alone. Try to get my perspective back. Chill out. Okay?"

Leslye couldn't quite hide her disappointment, but she tried. "Sure, Harry," she said. "You take care of yourself. It'll all look better Monday morning. I'm sure there's nothing to worry about."

"Yeah, maybe not," said Harry. He left her office, closing the door behind him.

Immediately, Leslye dialed a number on her desk phone. She was irritated when she reached an electronic device instead of a human.

"Stupid machine," she said beneath her breath. Then, into the phone, she said, "Yeah, it's me. Call me at home when you get in, no matter how late."

Then she hung up the phone and chewed at the edges of her expensive manicure.

. . . .

175

It was 2:45 a.m. by the digital bedside clock when Leslye's cell phone vibrated with a loud clatter on the nightstand and she writhed across silk sheets to answer it.

"Hello," she said, and looked at the clock while listening to the caller. "Well, it's about time. Listen, I think we'd better pay Harry a visit first thing in the morning. This thing could blow up in our faces if we're not careful. Meet me at the marina at nine thirty."

Without giving the other party a chance to argue, Leslye hung up and went back to sleep.

. . . .

Dinner Key Marina, Coconut Grove, Florida
The Day of the Explosion

A silver Bentley pulled in and parked beside the black Jaguar sedan in the yacht basin parking lot. The Jaguar disgorged Leslye Larrimore, who immediately approached a younger man, in Ostrich-skin boots, who angled out of the Bentley.

Attorney Larrimore slung her Louis Vuitton briefcase over her shoulder and extended her hand to the man. He shook her hand perfunctorily before shoving his soft, manicured hands into his pockets, ruining the perfect drape of his linen Euro-style slacks. "Where's Pace? It's hot out here," he said.

Leslye focused her practiced charm at him and assured, "It'll be cooler on the boat."

"It would be cooler in your *office*," he muttered. "This is what I get for kowtowing to Harry Pace. I know you like him, Leslye, but let's face it, Harry is a certifiable kook."

Leslye touched the man's elbow and steered him toward the nearby pier.

"Where are we meeting him?" he asked, scanning the yachts lining both sides of the long, floating pier.

"Out there," Leslye pointed to a sailing vessel moored a hundred yards out into the bay.

"Of course we are," the man sighed.

Together they walked to the end of the central pier, where Leslye flagged down a marina employee in a Zodiac pontoon runabout. In moments the Zodiac had pulled up directly before the couple, and it's pilot helped them board the twelve-foot inflatable.

Leslye negotiated the pier-to-craft transfer with amazing poise even in a pencil skirt and high heels. The man in Ostrich boots removed his suit jacket and loosened his collar; he produced a monogrammed handkerchief and wiped perspiration from his head and face.

"Can we hurry this along, please," he said, commanding rather than asking.

Leslye's smile never faltered. She gestured to the pilot, and the Zodiac putt-putted away from the pier.

Minutes later the runabout, with its company of three, was about halfway between the shore and an out-moored sailing yacht with "Helen" in florid gold lettering on the stern. Leslye delved into her briefcase and lifted her cell phone.

"I'll just let Harry know we're here," she said.

Seconds later, the faint ring of a telephone could be heard coming from the Helen – and a deafening blast vaporized the yacht in a cloud of fire and debris.

Concussion from the explosion rocked the Zodiac. Leslye, her companion, and the marina employee hid their faces from the glaring flames and covered their heads from falling debris. The marina employee shouted "Mister Pace!" and moved as if to dive overboard and attempt a rescue.

Leslye stopped him with a hand on his shoulder, a look, and a wag of her head. Harry Pace, master of the good ship Helen, was no more. Nothing remained but a burning oil slick, black smoke, and floating shards of teak decking.

"You absolutely sure Harry was on that boat?" said the man in Ostrich boots. His voice held amazingly little emotion.

Leslye kept her eyes on the burning, sinking, unrecognizable mass of wood and fiberglas. She nodded.

The man looked back toward his parked car then glanced at his diamond-studded Rolex watch. "Okay. We're done here, then. I need to get back to work."

CHAPTER THREE – THE MORTUARY

Miami—Tuesday Evening
Four Days After the Explosion

Lithgow Funeral Home was an elegant building with white marble columns facing a circular driveway bounded by well-manicured box hedges. It resembled the front entrance at the Academy Awards, with wealthy mourners arriving in their chauffeur-driven gas guzzlers. Everyone who was anyone simply must be seen at the viewing of the late Harry Pace, and they must be seen at their best. The jewelry had come out of the safe deposit boxes for this one. The glittering ladies and their silk-penguin escorts craved cameras, and the local media did not disappoint.

Inside a crowded reception room lined with flowers, sterling candelabra flanked a closed casket. An exquisite oil painting of Harry Pace rested on an easel at one end of the casket. A few of the attendees amused themselves speculating as to how many inches, or ounces, of Harry were actually inside the casket, which must have cost as much as a Space Shuttle.

Sylvie Pace, young, blonde and beautiful (of course) in a thousand-dollar simple black dress, graciously shook the hands of whatever "mourners" stopped by her chair to pay respects.

Dan Stern sat attentively on Sylvie's right. He was a little older, a lot taller and darker, and a little less beautiful than Sylvie. But Dan always cut a fine figure in his expensive suits and hand-made Ostrich-skin boots.

Together Sylvie and Dan were the South Florida equivalent of royalty, on glorious display.

Leslye Larrimore, looking strained despite her professionally applied makeup, caught Dan's eye from somewhere in the crowd. He gave her a "come hither" gesture. After a few moments of careful maneuvering, Les arrived at Dan's chair. He rose to whisper to her.

"Stay with Sylvie a minute, will you?" said Dan. "I've gotta go outside for a smoke."

"Nasty habit," Leslye told him before taking her seat in the chair he had vacated.

"Yeah, so's Valium," was his snarky reply.

Leslye sent him an overly sweet smile, and Dan headed for the nearest exit.

Walt McGurk's red pickup with yellow doors rolled into the funeral home parking lot just as Dan emerged with an unlit cigarette in his mouth. Dan must have recognized the truck, because Walt stepped out of the driver's side door to find his path blocked by Dan Stern, casually lighting a cigarette.

"Thought you had quit," Walt said. "Smart folks have."

Dan scowled at Walt's black western shirt, black jeans, black Stetson hat, and black boots. "You've got no business here, Dogpatch," said Dan. "Why don't you save Sylvie and the rest of us some embarrassment and just mosey on back to the ranch." He blew a smoke ring directly into Walt's face.

Walt dismissed Dan with a look and walked past him toward the funeral home entrance.

Dan tossed his freshly lit cigarette to the ground and followed. At the door, Dan grabbed Walt's shoulder and pulled him aside. "What are you trying to do!?"

"Just tryin' to pay my respects," said Walt.

"Respect! You and Harry fought like alley cats. Neither one of you ever showed any 'respect' to the other one."

"I didn't come to see Harry. I came to see Sylvie."

Walt shook off Dan's grip and entered the building. Once inside, he worked his way through the throng toward Sylvie's chair. The high-society, glammed-to-the-max crowd scorned his horse-ranch attire with looks and whispered comments. Walt ignored them and presented himself before Sylvie's chair. He removed his hat, took her hand, and pulled her up to walk with him to the closed casket.

They gave no greetings to one another but stood together in silence beside the easel displaying Harry's portrait.

Sylvie unconsciously leaned against Walt. When she sniffled, he folded her against him in a brotherly hug.

Gently, Walt told her, "Whatever's in that box, it ain't Harry. Y'hear me? Harry ain't here. You need to remember that."

"I know," replied Sylvie between weepy hiccups. "The preacher said the same thing. I guess Daddy's with Mama now. In heaven."

Walt smiled to himself. "Well, I don't know if I'd give Harry quite that much credit."

Across the room, Dan Stern joined Les Larrimore in watching Walt comfort Sylvie over the casket. Leslye whispered, "I thought you said she hated him."

Dan shrugged. "That's what she says. Avoids him and his place like the plague."

"Well, Danny boy, you better be sure she's had her shots. That plague looks contagious to me," said Leslye.

Dan's expression turned anxious. He moved toward Sylvie and Walt. Coming to Sylvie's side a moment later, Dan gently extricated her from Walt's arms and tenderly ushered her away. "Come sit down, sweetheart," Dan told her. "You look a little woozy."

Dan lovingly helped Sylvie into her chair. Leslye sat in the adjacent seat. Dan said to Sylvie, "Les will get you something to drink." He glanced at the lady lawyer meaningfully. "Right, Les?"

Leslye stood and found herself staring into the shirtfront of Walt McGurk, who had followed Sylvie and Dan. "I'll be right back; you just rest, dear," Leslye told Sylvie. Looking up at Walt towering over them, she said, "Good night, Mister McGurk. Thank you for coming." She stepped around him and left in search of a beverage.

Walt scanned the room. Sylvie was surrounded by elegant strangers and watchdogged by Dan Stern. Walt shoved his Stetson onto his head and ambled toward the exit.

Halfway there he stopped, decided he was not leaving, and marched briskly back to Sylvie's chair. He elbowed his way to her and, when Dan refused to yield a place to sit, Walt squatted on the floor in front of her. This put Walt on Sylvie's eye level, and he pinned her with his eyes like a lepidopterist skewers a butterfly.

"Sylvie, you know half of my ranch is yours now. Harry's half," Walt said.

"I guess so."

"Well, if you're in a bind, I'll buy you out fair and square. Cash on the barrelhead."

Dan said, "Really, McGurk! I don't think this is the time—"

"I'm talkin' to Sylvie," Walt said, cutting Dan short.

Sylvie didn't feel like discussing business at all, and certainly not while Walt and Dan were going at each other in front of the jet set. "Can't we discuss this later?" Sylvie said to Walt. "I mean, it's not like I need the money."

Walt's mouth moved as if he would argue with her, but he realized the room had gone silent. The "mourners" all seemed to be staring at him. He stood abruptly, withered the room with a look, and strode for the door.

Leslye arrived with a cup of water for Sylvie. Dan gave Les his chair, and he left to follow Walt, saying to the ladies, "I'll just make sure he finds his way out."

Les urged Sylvie to drink, but Sylvie merely held the cup and watched the door through which Walt and Dan had gone. Leslye patted Sylvie's shoulder and said, "It's all right, darling. Don't let Harry's pet jailbird upset you."

"Harry's what?"

"Jailbird," said Les. "Everybody knows Harry got him out of jail and set him up in that horse-breeding business." Bitterness tainted her voice as she continued, "One of your mother's charity cases, I expect. Harry never learned to tell her no."

Sylvie looked at Les in absolute confusion.

"Honey, they say McGurk killed a man," Les told her. "After all these years, I can't believe you never knew. I thought Harry would've told you all about it."

Stunned, Sylvie gulped the water from the cup like an android. Without looking at Leslye, Sylvie handed her the empty cup. "I guess Harry and I never really talked much," Sylvie said.

Out in the parking lot, Walt was reaching to open the door of his truck when Dan Stern wedged himself between Walt and his goal. "Who do you think you are?" Dan sneered from six inches away.

"Harry's partner, Slick Face. Who do you think you are?" Walt responded.

"Les and I were Harry's partners, Dogpatch. Real partners, in multi-million-dollar joint ventures, not some two-bit horse farm in Podunk Holler. You're not a business partner, you're a joke."

Without raising his voice, Walt responded, "And you're a brass-plated thief."

Dan took a good Ivy League swing at Walt, but Walt sidestepped it and landed a solid back-alley uppercut to Dan's jaw. Dan went down on one knee and stayed there, wiping blood from a split lip.

Standing over Dan with his fists poised for more, Walt said, "Harry never had to worry about finding my hands in his pockets. Tell me, did Harry kill himself when he learned you two had stole him broke, or did you blow him away because he caught you at it?"

"It was a gas leak," Dan insisted, favoring his swollen, bleeding lip. "An accident. Happens every day. You can ask the police, the Marine Patrol, the coroner, anybody." A new gleam entered Dan's eyes, and he smiled wickedly. "But you won't. You don't think I murdered Harry. This," he gestured at the two of them, "is all a smoke screen to hide how you tried to get Harry's half of the ranch from Sylvie before Harry's body was even in the grave. Y'know, if I were going to be suspicious of anybody, Dogpatch, I'd be suspicious of you. We both know you're capable of murder, don't we?"

Walt moved as if he wanted to kick Dan's perfectly capped teeth down his throat, but he decided against it. He swung into his truck instead.

As the truck roared out of the lot, Dan stood and wiped his face with his Hermes handkerchief. Then he dusted the knees of his trousers and re-entered the funeral home.

END OF SAMPLE CHAPTERS
OF
SYLVIE'S COWBOY
BY
IRIS CHACON

SCHIFFLEBEIN'S FOLLY

Lloyd plans to start his own business, find and marry Miss Right, and – most of all – adopt six special-needs kids. Simple.

Except that corrupt politicians are sabotaging his business, the only candidate for Miss Right is engaged to someone else, and the adoptions are on hold because people think Lloyd might be crazy.

Lloyd seems even crazier when supernatural occurrences – like talking teapots – suddenly proliferate in his life.

Will he ever become a husband and father?

PROLOGUE: THE STUDIO

In the oldest and most perfect pottery studio in the universe, the walls glowed with ethereal light. The ceiling was high enough to be hidden by clouds. The only flaw in the studio's splendor was its single door, which was narrow, wooden, plain, and scarred. Through that door bustled a peculiar, small person sporting a cocked stovepipe hat. He closed the door and waited politely for the Potter to acknowledge him.

The diminutive visitor looked like a 19th century sidewalk newsboy, or he might have been a taller-than-average leprechaun. Truly, he could be both, either, or neither, as the situation demanded. He was older than he looked by several million years, but he could pass for middle-aged on any planet. His name was Orkney.

185

Orkney watched in silence as the Potter fashioned a teapot and then its lid. He watched the Potter paint the raw clay and then set the two pieces into a kiln for firing.

A glance at the nearby workbench revealed a freshly painted vase, an urn, some candelabra, cups, saucers, a platter, but no other teapots.

When a minute had passed, or it may have been a year or a decade (time having no meaning in the studio), the Potter lifted the fired teapot from the kiln and set about painting a face upon it. Orkney neither moved nor spoke during all that time.

"Good to see you, Orkney," said the Potter, at whose smile Orkney nearly floated with happiness.

"You called, Guvnor?" Orkney said, sounding like a London street urchin—which he could be if called upon.

"Time to go to work again, my son," the Potter said, putting the finishing touches on the teapot's facial features. "It's been thirty-two years, seven months, four days, and six hours since the last job, by human reckoning."

"Human. So it's to be earth again, sir?"

The Potter put down his paintbrush and stepped back to evaluate his creation. He produced a neon green card from among the folds of his robe and flipped the card toward Orkney. Orkney remained absolutely still while the card wafted across the room and lodged itself securely in the band of his stovepipe hat. "That's the name and address where you'll deliver this teapot," said the Potter.

Orkney retrieved the card from his hatband and read it. He blew out air. "Coo! This bloke? They think 'e's bonkers already, Guv. This'll get 'im locked up for sure!"

"Just deliver the teapot."

Orkney looked at the teapot with its newly painted face. "But i's still wet!"

A gust of wind swept through the studio, billowing fabrics and rustling small items on the workbench.

"It's dry now," the Potter said. He placed the lid on the teapot then handed the pot to Orkney.

As Orkney accepted the teapot, it grinned and winked at the Potter.

CHAPTER 1: THE DELIVERY

Lloyd had a philosophy: If it ain't broke, don't fix it. If it ain't on clearance (defined as at least 70 percent off), don't buy it. If it's less than 50 years old, it's too good to get rid of. If it's more than 50 years old, it's an antique and therefore too valuable to get rid of. It was a blessing that Lloyd had never married because his philosophy probably would have driven some poor female to commit murder sooner or later.

That's not to say Lloyd was undesirable as a man. Indeed, women above the age of 50 found him adorable and wanted to mother him. Women in their 40s found him polite, attentive, an excellent listener, and the perfect date for weddings, graduations, awards ceremonies, even funerals. Thirty-something ladies felt he wasn't career-driven enough, but he had a respectable investment portfolio and a cute butt. Twenty-somethings at the gym on Lloyd's workout days sent text messages to their friends about his great body— sometimes they even posted Lloyd videos on YouTube.

Despite his positive attributes, however, Lloyd had reached the age of thirty-two years, seven months, four days, and six hours without finding Miss Right and converting her into Mrs. Lloyd Schifflebein. Yes, Schifflebein. A surname decidedly lacking romance in addition to being difficult to spell and way too long a signature for checks and the backs of credit cards.

Supposing Miss Right were willing to overlook the awkward appellation, there was one other impediment to wedded bliss. Lloyd devoted his whole life to his children. Children he didn't yet actually have, but he was working on it. He had been working on it all his life. He had filed his first formal application to adopt on his 20th birthday, having been turned away on his 18th and 19th. This devotion to his as-yet-unadopted children led many people to deduce that Lloyd Schifflebein was crazy. Big and strong, sure. Cute, maybe, but loony nonetheless.

On the afternoon of Orkney's mission to Lloyd's house, Lloyd had laid aside his carpentry tools, locked his woodworking shop, and settled in the kitchen to brew a cup of tea and make an important telephone call. An ancient teakettle on the old Kenmore stove began to bubble and then whistle, blowing steam. Lloyd was lifting the kettle from the burner when his doorbell rang, startling him into dropping the kettle, which shattered into snowflake-size pieces on the tile floor. Lloyd had never seen stainless steel behave that way. It should have been dented or bent, but shattered? And where was the water? How weird.

Lloyd bent to pick up the mess, but the doorbell clanged again. He sighed and stepped over the debris on his way to answer the door.

He opened his front door to find Orkney on his threshold with a brown box in hand, clipboard under one arm, and pencil behind one ear.

"Delivery for Schifflebein," said Orkney. "Sign 'ere, if ya please, Guvnor." Orkney offered Lloyd the clipboard and pencil. Lloyd signed, then he exchanged the clipboard and pencil for Orkney's brown box.

"Well, g'day, Guvnor, and good luck."

Abruptly, thunder boomed out of a clear sky.

Orkney startled and glanced heavenward. He removed his hat respectfully and backed away from the door, keeping one eye on the heavens.

"No! Not luck, sir. I didn't mean luck, sir. I meant to say, uh, Lor' bless ya. G'day and Lor' bless ya, sir."

Lloyd, too, examined the clear skies and even held out his open hand to check for precipitation, but there was none. He turned to thank the strange little man, but Orkney had simply disappeared. Lloyd stepped outside the door and glanced up and down the street, but there was no sign of a delivery truck or driver. More weirdness. What a day. Shaking his head, Lloyd returned to his kitchen with his brown box.

He left the box on the counter, swept up and discarded the remains of his erstwhile teakettle, and walked down the hall to his home office to make his phone call. He opened a four-inch-thick file folder on his desk, found a number, and punched the digits into his phone.

"May I speak with Mrs. Walken, please?" he asked the answering receptionist. "Retired? But she couldn't have been more than 50! ... Oh, really. Well, she sure didn't sound 62. My goodness."

He paged quickly through the thick file and found his answer. "Wow, I guess it has been, goodness, twelve years now that she's been handling my file. ... Schifflebein, yes. You know my case? ... Really! Everybody, huh. ... Well, do you know who's handling my file now that Mrs. Walken has retired? ... Uh-huh. ... Uh-huh. ... Well, would you please ask whoever draws the short straw to call me? ... Yeah, that's still my number. You have an amazing memory. ... Really! Taped to the desk. Goodness. ... Thank you very much, then. I'll wait for your call, her call, or his call, somebody's call. ... Right. 'Bye."

Lloyd put down the phone, slumped in his chair with long legs extended before him. A black-and-white rabbit hopped through the office door, across Lloyd's ankles, and onward to the futon against the opposite office wall.

"Montalban, don't eat my bed," Lloyd said absently. The rabbit reversed course, crossed Lloyd's ankles going the other direction, and left the room.

After several minutes of staring at nothing, Lloyd slapped his knees as if encouraging himself. He rose and returned to the kitchen, where he removed a paring knife from the cutlery drawer and proceeded to open Orkney's brown box. He lifted the brand new teapot and placed it on the stove with its brightly colored face visible from the center of the room. "Goodness, this is providential," he said. "Who sent you?"

The teapot didn't answer, and there was no return address on the brown box. In fact, there was no address at all on the brown box. Lloyd turned the box over and around, but it was blank on all sides. "My goodness," Lloyd murmured.

At the Department of Children and Families, the receptionist delivered a Pepto-pink message slip to the desk of a supervisor. "Walken's nutty guy called," the receptionist said. "Who do I give it to?"

"I'll take it," the supervisor said, and rose from her chair to take the message in hand.

The receptionist returned to her desk, and the supervisor walked down an alley between cubicles to the lair of Hepzibah Stoner, Social Worker Extraordinaire.

Stoner was the unofficial hit-woman of DepChilFam (as she liked to call it, having become accustomed to such amalgamated nomenclature while serving in the United States Marine Corps). Stoner had the compassion of Florence Nightingale, the relentless determination of Indiana Jones, and, sadly, the face and physique of Winston Churchill.

The supervisor leaned into Stoner's cubicle and placed the phone message on the desk. "Kook call," said the supervisor. "Walken strung him along for twelve years hoping he'd give up, but he doesn't get it. Name's Snicklebean, or something like that. Everybody's talked to him at one time or another, but nobody's had the guts to just tell him no and put him out of his misery. Something about the guy seems to turn people soft. Find the file. Go see him. Tell him to get lost, and close the file."

"You got it," said Hepzibah Stoner. "Snicklebean is history."

CHAPTER 2: THE PLAN

Lloyd had been working for the Miami-Dade County Parks and Recreation Department for almost as long as he had been applying to adopt kids. On the official civil service rolls his position was Facilities Maintenance Technician, Level III, but he simply told people he was a handyman.

His best friend since childhood was one of his co-workers (a Facilities Maintenance Technician, Level II), a black woman named Rembrandt Jackson. If Lloyd didn't love her so much, he would have envied Remmy. She had five children under the age of 12.

On the day after Lloyd's file was assigned to Hit-Woman Hepzibah, Lloyd—unaware that he had been targeted—was meeting his pal, Remmy, for lunch. They parked their County truck at the Rolando Castillo Memorial Park and walked across the grass that Lloyd would be mowing after they finished eating.

Remmy headed straight for the only bench that was nestled in a shady patch. Other people, sitting on other benches around the small park, were courting sunstroke in the Miami summer heat. The only shady bench was vacant only because of the large "Wet Paint" sign taped to it.

Remmy reached the bench slightly ahead of Lloyd, deftly flipped aside the sign, and sat down.

Lloyd joined her on the bench, but he could not condone dishonesty. "Remmy, please. 'Wet Paint'?"

"It will be," said Remmy. "Right after I finish my lunch."

She dug in her ottoman-size thermal lunch box and from it produced plastic bags of carrots, celery, cherry tomatoes, cauliflower, and broccoli florets, all sliced into bite-size pieces. She withdrew a large mixing bowl from the bottom of the lunch box, dumped all the veggies into the bowl, then emptied an entire bottle of blue cheese dressing on top of it all. She set a can of Diet Pepsi next to the empty dressing bottle on the bench beside her.

Eating a simple brown-bagged tuna sandwich at his end of the not-yet-wet bench, Lloyd watched with mild interest as Remmy assembled her salad. "Still on your diet, I see," he remarked."

"I sho' am," Remmy boasted. "I bet I've lost a pound and a half this month alone. Imagine if I can stay on it for a whole year. You want a brownie?" She held up a plastic bag of brownies.

"No, thanks. You can have mine."

"Fine then. You let me know if ya change yer mind. I'll save yo' brownie for last."

Lloyd reached across the bench and picked up the empty blue cheese dressing bottle. He read the label. "This says 140 calories per serving."

"Yeah, 140 calories is nuthin'. I can have 300 calories for lunch, and ever'body knows raw vegetables is mostly water, so I'm good."

"Remmy, there are eight servings in this bottle, and you used the whole bottle," he said.

"Oh," she said. "That's bad. Guess I'll skip the brownies. That oughta make up the difference."

"Good plan," he said, tossing the salad dressing bottle into the nearby recycling bin.

"'Course, I can still eat *yo'* brownie," Remmy reasoned. "It's only my own dessert calories that count. Nobody can be penalized for somebody else's dessert calories."

Lloyd nodded. He had no response for Remmy's nutritional logic, and he valued their friendship too much to risk a faux pas with regard to a woman's weight. All males worth their testosterone knew what a minefield that topic could be.

They relaxed and enjoyed their shady lunch together in the comfortable silence born of many years' camaraderie.

After some minutes Remmy said, "Still goin' through wid it?"

"Mwhawf?" said Lloyd around a mouthful of tuna sandwich.

"The bid."

"Ympfh."

"And you'll actually quit this glamorous, high-payin' job?" she teased.

Lloyd swallowed his last bite of sandwich and threw his trash into the appropriate receptacles. He produced a pad and pencil from a large pocket in his cargo pants and began sketching as they talked.

"Have to quit," he said. "Conflict of interest."

"Heckuva big risk," she said. "I just don't believe you've really thought this through."

"Remmy, I'll be able to work from home. Be there for my kids." Lloyd studied the playground nearby, where a few children were playing. He began drawing the playground.

Remmy continued eating for three bites before commenting, "Yo' kids. You know what I think 'bout dat."

"I'm not getting married," he said.

"How about cloning? Cloning's coming right along these days, according to the news."

"I don't want sheep," he said.

"Yeah, and I've noticed you're the perfect candidate for adoption," Remmy said sarcastically. "No wife, no parents, no wealth, no college degree, no perfectly good civil service job after tomorrow, and—oh, did I mention?—you're nuts. No offense. It's what we all love about you. But, honey, dey gone give kids to Jack The Ripper before dey give 'em to you. Dey ain't never even come to yo' house for the follow-up interview."

Lloyd stopped drawing. "Yes they have—or at least, they will. A social worker is coming to the house at 5:30 this evening. Her name is," he slid a folded slip of paper from a pocket and opened it. "Stoner. Hepzibah Stoner. Five-thirty tonight." He folded and pocketed the paper with a triumphant grin.

He leaned toward Remmy and showed her his drawing of the playground. He had captured the movement and whimsy of the children climbing the weathered slide and jungle gym.

Remmy looked at the sketch, and smiled to let him know she liked it. She handed it back to him, shaking her head. Then she lifted her eyes skyward and said, "Lawd, have mercy on dis poor, sweet, crazy soul," tilting her head toward Lloyd so God would be sure to take her meaning.

Across town, in a much better neighborhood, the newly landscaped Commissioner Rosa Garcia-Katz Park sprawled under the Florida sun. Garcia-Katz Park was the jewel in the crown of the Miami-Dade County Parks and Recreation Department (ex-Marine Hepzibah Stoner would have said ParRecDep). Jogging paths wound through the landscape, a Frisbee field was set aside for dogs and their owners, and the County was about to accept bids for a new design in playground equipment.

The Garcia-Katz Park playground would be the pilot project for potential renovation or replacement of deteriorating old playground equipment at all the County's parks. The lucky contractor who entered the low bid for the pilot project might eventually earn millions by the time all the parks were finished—a task that was scheduled for completion over the coming decade.

Garcia-Katz Park was named in honor of one of Miami-Dade's County Commissioners. Rosa Garcia-Katz supported ParRecDep (though she didn't call it that) and, in fact, lived in the posh neighborhood surrounding the park that bore her name.

On the day Lloyd and Remmy lunched together in a distant and less affluent part of town, Commissioner Garcia-Katz was jogging through "her" park. Jogging toward her from the opposite end of the park was Dr. Arthur Frankel, psychiatrist, investor, and campaign contributor. The two joggers did not acknowledge one another, but when they approached an intersection of paths, they both turned so that they were running side-by-side.

"Evening, Arthur," the Commissioner said, without turning her head in his direction.

"Commissioner," said Frankel, also looking straight ahead.

"Bids are due by noon tomorrow," she said.

"Ours will be delivered by 8:30 a.m.," Frankel responded. "The same messenger will be delivering our group's campaign fund check to your secretary."

They continued to jog, keeping their eyes on the path before them. Commissioner Garcia-Katz smiled as if counting the campaign money already. Then her brow furrowed as she voiced a concern, "You're sure your group's design meets the specs?"

Frankel snorted. "How should I know? I'm not an architect. The people we hire to build the thing will take care of that."

"They'd better, or your whole group will not only be looking for a new tax shelter, you'll be looking for a good defense attorney."

Frankel smiled, totally at ease. "Look around you, Commissioner. When's the last time you saw children actually playing in a public park in this neighborhood? They're all at lacrosse practice or violin lessons or sailing or ballet or whatever. No child is ever going to be endangered by this park's equipment because no child in this neighborhood is ever going to use it. So, don't you worry about what kind of pilot playground we build. You just make sure that we're the ones who build it."

Moments later the jogging path diverged into two separate paths, and the two joggers headed in different directions without ever looking at each other. From a distance, nobody would know they had been talking at all.

END OF SAMPLE CHAPTERS
OF
SCHIFFLEBEIN'S FOLLY
BY
IRIS CHACON

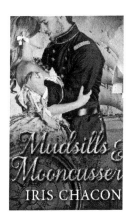

MUDSILLS &

MOONCUSSERS

During the Civil War, in Key West – southernmost city in the divided nation – a Northern spy searches for a Southern saboteur. He only hopes – despite evidence to the contrary - that she will not turn out to be the very woman with whom he has fallen in love.

CHAPTER 1

1862

Sergeant Jules Pfifer, a career Army man, marched his patrol briskly through the evening heat toward a tall wooden house on the corner of Whitehead Street and Duval Street. Atop the house was perched a square cupola surrounded by the sailor-carved balustrades called gingerbread. These porches, just large enough for one or two persons to stand and observe the sea from the rooftop, were known as widows' walks. From this particular widow's walk an illegal Confederate flag flaunted its red stars and bars against the clear Key West sky.

The soldiers in Union blue marched smartly through the gate in the white picket fence, up the front steps, and in at the front door—which opened before them as if by magic.

"Evenin', Miz Lowe," Sergeant Pfifer said, without breaking stride, to the woman who had opened the door.

"Evenin', Sergeant," the lady of the house answered, unperturbed.

On the Lowe house roof, the stars and bars were whipped from their post; they disappeared from sight just as the soldiers, clomping and puffing and sweat-stained, arrived atop the stairway. Pfifer and another man crowded onto the widow's walk. Consternation wrinkled the soldiers' faces when they found no Confederate flag, only 17-year-old Caroline Lowe, smiling sweetly.

...

In the twilight, the three-story brick trapezoid of Fort Zachary Taylor loomed castle-like over the sea waves. It stood on its own 63-acre shoal, connected to the island of Key West by a narrow 1000-foot causeway. The fort had taken 21 years to build and was plagued by constant shortages of men and material as well as outbreaks of deadly yellow fever.

Yankee sentries paced between the black silhouettes of cannon pointed seaward. Firefly lights of campfires and lanterns sparkled on the parade ground and among the Sibley tents huddled on shore at the base of the causeway.

Midway between the fort and Caroline Lowe's flagpole, on the tin roof of a three-story wooden house, behind the gingerbread railing of another widow's walk, two athletic, handsome youngsters stood close together, blown by the wind. Twenty-year-old Richard scanned the sea with a spyglass. Joe, an inch shorter than Richard, kept one hand atop a floppy hat the wind wanted to steal.

Richard found something interesting to the east. He handed over the spyglass and pointed Joe toward the same point on the horizon. Joe searched, then zeroed in.

"Some rascal's laid a false light over on Boca Chica," Richard said, referring to the smaller island just north of Key West. "Come on!"

They tucked the spyglass into a hollow rail of the widow's walk and hastened down the stairs.

...

On neighboring Boca Chica island, night blanketed the beach. A hunched figure tossed a branch onto a blazing bonfire then slunk away into the darkness. Pine pitch popped and crackled in the fire, adding its sweet aroma to the tang of the salty breeze coming off the sea.

...

Inside a warehouse on Tift's Wharf, all shapes and sizes of kegs, boxes, and wooden crates towered in jagged heaps. Sickly yellow light from a sailor's lantern sent quivering shadows across the stacks. A spindly boy of 15, Joseph Porter, kept watch through a crack in the door.

On the floor a dozen teenaged boys hunkered down, whispering. Richard sneaked in from the rear of the building to join them. Behind him, out of the light and keeping quiet, came Joe.

Porter hissed, "Mudsills comin'!"

The whispered buzz of conversation halted. Someone doused the light. Bodies thumped to the floor as the boys took cover.

Outside, footsteps ground into the gravelly dirt of the street. Four Yankee soldiers, the source of the boys' concern, completed a weary circuit of the dark dockside buildings. They were Pennsylvania farm boys not much older than the Key West boys hiding inside.

The southern boys would have been surprised to know that the Yankees in the street were not technically "mudsills;" that was the name given to northern factory workers who lived crowded together in dirt-floored shacks along muddy streets. Still, the word was applied to all the Yankee enemies, just as the northern boys would have called Key West residents "mooncussers," as if they all were pirates.

Native born citizens of Key West referred to themselves as Conchs, a term dating back to the 1780s immigration of British Loyalists from the Bahamas. A large shellfish called a conch was plentiful in the local waters and became a staple of the pioneers' diet.

On Tift's Wharf one of the Pennsylvania soldiers said something in Dutch-German, and the others murmured agreement. They sounded homesick. One slapped a mosquito on his neck then turned up his collar, grumbling.

In front of the warehouse the soldiers stopped beside a barrel set to catch rainwater running off the tin roof during storms. They loosened their woolen tunics and dipped their handkerchiefs into the water, laving themselves, trying in vain to ease the steamy agony of tropical heat.

Inside, the wide-eyed Conch boys held their breath, listening to the sounds from the water barrel outside. Joseph Porter trembled, perspired, and stared cross-eyed at a gigantic mosquito making itself at home on the end of his nose. He tried to raise one hand quietly to chase the brute away, but his elbow nudged a crate of bottles. Glass tinkled. The boys froze.

Outside, a soldier started at the sound and snatched up his weapon. *"Vas ist das?"*

The other soldiers were less concerned. They were hot, tired, and not looking for trouble.

"Rats," one said. "These pirate ships are full of them. Let's go back to the ice house. It's cooler."

The sweat-covered Conch boys heard the receding footsteps of the Yankees. Long, sweltering seconds later, Porter crept to his crack in the door and risked a peek. "It's all right. They're gone."

Red-haired William Sawyer lit the lantern.

A bigger boy, Marcus Oliveri, stepped forward and cuffed Porter smartly. "Porter, you imbecile!"

"Here now, Marcus!" said William. "He didn't mean to."

Oliveri returned to his place in the circle of boys forming around the lantern. "I don't fancy getting arrested or maybe shot because Porter can't abide getting mosquito bit for his country!"

"I'm sorry," said Porter. "It was an accident."

"Let's just forget it," urged William. "Let's finish up and get out of here before they come back. Now, the English schooner leaves for Nassau tomorrow morning. Richard and

Marcus and Alfred and me will be on it. The rest of you know what to do to cover for us."

An older boy with a thick Bahamian accent, Alfred Lowe, shook his finger under the nose of a friend. "And you, Bogy Sands, stay away from my sister while I'm gone, you hear me?"

Richard looked surprised. He thought he and Caroline Lowe had an unspoken agreement. "Caroline? Bogy!"

"You ain't engaged to her, Thibodeaux," said Bogy.

William Sawyer's hair flashed the same fiery color as the lamplight when he reached across the circle to separate Richard and Bogy. "That's enough of that! Let's not be fighting each other. God willing, we'll all be soldiers of the Seventh Florida Regiment within the year. Any questions?"

All around the circle the boys murmured in the negative.

"Let's get home then, and be ready when the call comes," William said.

The boys scrambled away. Joe and Richard were the last to leave, watching for Yankee patrols while the others sneaked out.

Joe complained, "I'll probably break my neck walking around in your boots. You got such big feet, Wretched! I had to stuff the toes with rags."

"You just keep that hat on and stay out of Papa's way. You'll do fine," Richard replied.

As they moved to leave the warehouse, Richard put an arm around Joe's shoulders and gave an encouraging squeeze.

...

In the Florida Straits between Key West and Cuba, just before dawn, two lithe, black fishermen reacted to the flare of a distress signal that arced upward in the eastern sky. One fisherman reached into the bilge of his craft and produced the empty pink-and-white spiraling shell of that large mollusk called a conch. He lifted the trumpet-size conch shell to his lips and blew a loud, hooting blast.

Seconds later on Tift's Wharf, a lookout in a wooden tower reacted to the distant conch horn, scanned the eastern horizon with a spyglass for barely an instant, then clanged the wreckers' bell and shouted to wake the whole island.

"Wreck asho-o-o-re! Wreck asho-o-o-re!"

Men of all sizes came running from every direction. Black men and white, old and young, in jerseys and loose short pants, they raced through the streets of Key West to the Jamaica sloops moored in the harbor. Every shopkeeper (save one, William Curry) left his store, every clergyman his church, every able-bodied homeowner his house. Quickly it became apparent that nearly every man in Key West, whatever else he might be, was a wrecker.

Men shouted, the bell clanged, the distant conch horn trumpeted. The race was on. Yankee soldiers, standing on the street corner, did well not to be trampled in the rush.

At Fort Taylor, blue-clad soldiers on the roof of the fort took note of the wreck and watched closely the activity in the harbor, ready to take action if necessary.

Aboard the moored schooner *Lady Alyce*, white-bearded, patriarchal Captain Elias Thibodeaux, regal in his double-breasted jacket, surveyed the scene with hawk's eyes. The *Lady Alyce*, at 50 feet and 136 tons, was a sleek topsail schooner with well-greased masts, coiled lines, and shining brightwork. She looked like she could outsail anything.

"Mister Simmons," the captain shouted.

The mate, Cataline Simmons, was a black Bahamian with the muscles and instincts of an experienced sailor and the accent of an Oxford professor. "Aye, sir!"

Thibodeau's eyes searched the wharf again, but it was no use. What he sought was not there. "Hoist the mains'l," he commanded.

Cataline, too, looked with concern at the wharf before executing the order.

"Today, Simmons!" bellowed the captain. "We'll leave him if we have to, but I will be first to bespeak that wreck!"

Cataline leapt into action, gesturing to four crewmen— three white, one black—who waited poised at their stations. "Aye, sir! Hoist the mains'l."

The three white crewmen set about their tasks quickly, skillfully. The small, wiry black man, Stepney Austin, hesitated. If Thibodeaux was king here, and he undoubtedly was, then Stepney Austin was the court jester. Monkeylike in his movements and Cockney in his speech, he could be the bane of Simmons' existence if he were not so brave and loyal.

"Cast off the docklines," said the captain.

Cataline threw Stepney a look. Stepney moved as if he had been waiting for just such an order.

The sail was filling; other boats were getting underway. Stepney cast off the bow lines and moved deliberately toward the stern, watching the wharf as did Cataline. Thibodeaux turned away and looked seaward, giving up on finding what he sought upon the wharf.

Then Joe, baggy in Richard's clothing and unsteady in Richard's boots, appeared at the far side of the wharf, running toward the *Lady Alyce*.

Stepney cried, "There he is!"

Thibodeaux did not look. "Cast off!"

Cataline lifted a cargo block hanging from the rigging nearby and, as he spoke, swung the block like a great pendulum out over the wharf. "Casting off. Aye, aye, sir."

Stepney was forced to comply, but it was in slow motion that he cast off the stern line.

Joe ran desperately to close the gap of several yards between Richard's reluctant boots and the departing schooner. When the cargo block swung toward Joe, Joe took full advantage of it by grabbing it and hanging on for dear life.

Stepney chanted, "Come on, come on!"

Joe's forward motion combined with the pendulum swing of the block to carry Joe, like a trapeze artist, across the chasm now yawning between schooner and wharf. Joe landed more-or-less flatfooted on the deck behind Captain Thibodeaux. Richard's floppy hat tumbled from Joe's head, followed by a cascade of unruly curls that reached halfway down her back.

CHAPTER 2

Stepney Austin lurched forward and opened his mouth, only to find Cataline Simmons's hand clapped across his face. Cataline gestured with a sidewise tilt of his head to the schooner across the harbor—the one flying the English flag—then glared disapproval at Joe and the errant hat.

Joe grabbed the hat, stuffed the telltale curls into it, and replaced it on her head.

Thibodeaux still did not look around. "Good morning, Richard. So good of you to join us. Now get aloft and find me that wreck."

"Aye, sir!" said Joe and climbed for the top of the mast. The other crewmen tackled their duties with renewed relish. Cataline and Stepney exchanged a look. The wrecking fleet departed, leaving behind the English schooner, with four young stow-aways on board, across the harbor.

...

On Pelican Shoal, near the edge of the Gulf Stream's warm current, the *St. Gertrude*, a 200-foot merchantman, sat at an odd angle, jarring, creaking, and shuddering. Waves whapped her sides and wind jangled her rigging. She had wedged her keel firmly aground. A dozen anxious crewmen lined the *St. Gertrude's* rail, watching the *Lady Alyce* approach, trailed by other wrecking sloops—though none within 300 yards of her.

It appeared that a young boy in floppy hat and baggy clothes stood at the helm of the *Lady Alyce*. The white-bearded, red-coated captain was an imposing figure as he stepped into the bow and hailed the grounded merchantman. "Ahoy, *St. Gertrude!*"

Aaron Matthews, a tall, well-built man in a brocade jacket, returned a lusty shout from the bridge of the merchantman. "Ahoy, yourself! Can we assist you?"

Thibodeaux smiled at the younger man's audacity. "Could you stand to lighten your load a bit?"

"Have you come to rob me, then?" replied Matthews.

"Naw! Naw, no need for that. We'll just bide here 'til the next tide breaks you up and take what's left. Or, we could pull you off, see you safe into Key West, and let the admiralty court decide who gets what."

The young captain of the *St. Gertrude* was considering his options when his arm was taken by a beautiful woman who came up behind him—an antebellum china doll, from the taffeta hoop skirt to the shiny hair piled high on her head, showing off her dainty dangling earrings. This was Lila Dauthier.

"You're not seriously thinking of allowing those ... those *mooncussers* to come aboard, are you, Aaron?" Lila simpered.

"I was, yes."

"But, sweetheart! Everyone knows they're no better than pirates. Vultures. They cause ships to wreck just so they can loot them."

Aaron fondled her earring and teased her with a smile. "They may have played a trick or two in their time, Lila my dove, but I can hardly blame them for this one, since I myself was at the helm. Someone must have distracted me."

Aaron had amused himself with Lila in the past, and they had renewed their acquaintance aboard the *St. Gertrude* in recent days, but in truth he found her shallow and annoying, regardless of her obvious physical charms. He was enough of a cad to use the ladies and discard them casually. He was enough of a gentleman that his paramours never felt his disinterest, never perceived him disrespectful. In every instance, his women felt he had been prevented from continuing their pleasant liaison by circumstances beyond his control. There was a war on, naturally.

Aboard the *Lady Alyce*, Captain Thibodeaux knew the other sloops were drawing closer, but his position as master of this wreck was secure. He took in the situation with a shrewd look and shouted to the stranded vessel, "*St. Gertrude!* Have we permission to come aboard?"

Lila gave Aaron her most persuasive pleading look, but his smile told her she had lost this argument.

"Very well," she said. "I shall be in my cabin—securing my valuables."

Aaron watched her leave the bridge, her gait calculated to keep his attention. Suddenly he was in an expansive mood. He called over the rail, "Come aboard, my friends! Do your worst!"

"On the contrary, sir," Thibodeaux shouted. "We shall, as always, do our best!"

Thibodeaux gestured to his crewmen, who moved to carry out his unspoken order. Joe, at the helm, worked the *Lady Alyce* close alongside the *St. Gertrude,* where crewmen tied her up.

While Joe concentrated on this maneuver, Captain Thibodeaux took a seat near the helm, and lit his pipe. He spoke for Joe's ears alone.

"Richard never saw the day he could make six knots through Dry Rocks in a wind like we had tonight. I don't know what shenanigans you two are about, Josephine Marie, but if you're fool enough to take Richard's place, I'll expect you to keep your hat on and carry Richard's share of the load. Is that clear?"

Joe swallowed hard. "Aye, aye, sir. Clear as a bell."

A trace of a smile showed behind Thibodeaux's beard and pipe as he rose to step away. "Your Mama'll kill you when you get home, I reckon. Don't suppose you'd tell me where Richard has taken himself off to? Courting Caroline Lowe, maybe?"

"I don't know exactly where he is this minute," Joe answered truthfully.

...

Miles away, in the Gulf Stream, the English schooner had left Key West harbor behind and was making excellent headway under full sail toward the Bahamas. Aboard were four Conch boys on their way to join the Confederate Army.

...

On the streets of Key West, a patrol of Yankee soldiers made its way under the glaring mid-day sun toward Tift's Wharf. Something atop one of the houses on Duval Street caught Sergeant Pfifer's eye. "Shades of 'Barbara Frietchie,' she's at it again!" the sergeant cried. "Come on!"

A gray-haired lady and her plumpish daughter sat on the wide front porch of the Lowe house, plying their knitting needles. The sergeant and his men trooped through the front gate, strode up the walk, climbed the porch steps, and proceeded directly to the front door. A black house servant, waiting inside the door, swung it open just before they could crash into it. The ladies on the porch took no notice of the procession.

"Mornin', Miz Lowe. Miz Euphemie," mumbled the sergeant in passing.

On the Lowe house rooftop, feisty Caroline Lowe stood next to an improvised flagpole wherefrom waved her homemade Confederate flag. She watched the soldiers disappear through the front door below her, headed her way. She began taking down the flag with practiced speed.

The sergeant led his men, huffing and puffing in their woolen blue jackets, up the interior stairs to the roof. "Today's the day, Miss Caroline," he muttered. "Today we've got you."

Sergeant Pfifer and his men emerged onto the widow's walk to find Caroline waving to an admiring Bogy Sands, who watched from the street below. No flag—and no place to hide a flag—anywhere in sight.

The sergeant looked at Caroline's long, full skirt, but abandoned that idea for numerous reasons. He looked over the widow's walk railing on all four sides. Nothing. He looked at empty-handed Bogy Sands in the street below. He gave up. He turned back and growled at his men in frustration, "Search the house!"

The men piled back downstairs, mumbling. One said, "We searched the house yesterday."

"We'll search it again today and every day until we find that blasted pennant! Good day, Miss Caroline."

The lady answered with a thick 'Brilander British accent, "Always a pleasure, Sergeant.

...

It was nearly dusk in Key West harbor when the wrecking fleet returned, crowding the anchorage. All around, boats were made fast, and weary sailors headed homeward on foot.

Joe left the *Lady Alyce* and was greeted on shore by Joseph Porter. Together they turned and looked at the empty mooring where the English schooner had been that morning.

"They made it, Joe!" said Porter. "They got away clean."

"Yeah," she said. "Now comes the hard part."

"Fightin' the Yankees!"

"Telling my mother."

CHAPTER 3

Minutes later, in the dusk at Fort Zachary Taylor, Colonel T.H. Good stood on the ramparts, 50 feet above Key West harbor and the Gulf of Mexico, observing the activities on Tift's Wharf through his spyglass. A noise attracted Colonel Good's attention—someone climbing the steps from the parade ground to the shadows behind him. The colonel did not turn to look at the newcomer.

"Matheson?" the colonel ventured.

"Matthews, sir," answered a deep voice from the shadows.

Colonel Good continued his observations, throwing his words over his shoulder. "Matthews, then. If I may say so, Lieutenant, you chose the devil's own way to get here. But for your encounter with Pelican Shoal, I might have had to arrest you for a blockade runner. A lot of help you'd be to me sitting in jail at Fort Jefferson."

"You would've had to catch me first." The silence lingered almost too long before Aaron added, "Sir."

Colonel Good lowered his spyglass and delivered an affectionate pat to a massive black cannon pointing toward the sea. "Lieutenant, if I thought there was a ghost of a chance we wouldn't catch you, I'd have blown you out of the water. And if I didn't, the Union Navy's blockade ships would. And if they didn't, the guns at Fort Jefferson would.

We are the gateposts to the Gulf, Lieutenant. Nobody gets into our yard without being seen by one or the other of us."

"May I beg the colonel's indulgence to continue this audience in the colonel's office?" asked Aaron.

"You may not. This wind keeps the infernal mosquitos at bay, and I am partial to these sunsets."

The western sky glowed orange, red, pink, and purple as the sun sank into the Gulf of Mexico. Colonel Good and his cannon loomed as black shapes between Aaron and the dying sun. Aaron leaned well back into the shadows.

The colonel broke the silence. "What did you think you were doing, Matthews?"

"My job, sir. The one I've been given, not the one I would have chosen. Sir."

"Yes, yes, I know. The ignobility of it all. And what in God's name did you think you would do if you had not grounded on Pelican? Go on to Mobile?"

"Perhaps I would've been welcome there. I thought they picked me for this job because of my social connections in Charleston. I could have visited the homes of Confederate supporters—maybe even officers and politicians. I might even have done some good. ... Sir."

The colonel scoffed. "Until they caught you and hauled you before a Rebel firing squad. Your work is here. You will forego martyrdom for the time being, Lieutenant."

Aaron came to his feet, but before he could turn away the colonel wheeled to face Aaron and laid his spyglass gently but firmly on Aaron's shoulder.

"Tell me what you saw in the harbor when you left Havana," the colonel said.

"A couple of English-built sloops, very fast I think, and one frigate with nasty looking cannon."

"And you are not concerned, Lieutenant?"

"Ending this war is my concern, Colonel, and wasting my time and talents on this godforsaken, out-of-the-way piece of rock is not my idea of the way to do it." Aaron acknowledged the increased pressure of the spyglass on his shoulder and slumped back into his seat in the shadows.

Colonel Good slapped his telescope shut. "You want to end this war? Food, gunpowder, clothing, shoes, tools, weapons—I've got a shipment of LeMat grapeshot revolvers sent from France for issue to Confederate solders—these are the things that will end this war. The South has to ship raw materials out and finished goods back in, just like breathing. We can strangle it."

"Be my guest," said Aaron. "You don't need me or whoever's in Havana harbor."

"Wrong. I need you *because* of whoever's in Havana harbor. Practically everyone one on this island has closer ties to Havana harbor than you have to your own mother."

Aaron's tone was ironic. "That goes without saying."

"I'm sorry. I didn't mean..."

"Permission to withdraw, sir. I need to see to housing myself with the locals."

Colonel Good nodded and seemed tired as he turned away. "Is your brother well, Lieutenant?"

"With General Floyd's troops near Sewell Mountain last I heard, sir. Just another loyal son of the Confederate state of South Carolina."

"At least it must be some consolation that while you're here you will not be shooting at him," said the colonel.

"Let's stop this war before someone else shoots at him, sir. How shall I contact you?"

The colonel sighed. "See the ship's chandler, Curry. But be discreet. Goodnight, uh, what name are you using, again?"

"Matthews, sir."

"Well, goodnight Matthews."

Aaron was halfway down the stone steps when the colonel called to him. "Aaron. Several of the officers and enlisted men have honorable intentions with regard to local ladies. I'll not tolerate complaints of defrauded debutantes. I shall expect you to exercise restraint."

"I'll try, sir." Aaron disappeared down the steps and across the darkness of the parade ground.

...

At dawn the next morning, Josephine Marie Thibodeaux entered her brother Richard's bedroom expecting to find it unoccupied. She beamed with surprise and delight when she beheld a slumbering form behind the mosquito netting. Thinking Richard had somehow regained his sanity and stayed away from yesterday's war-bound English schooner, she leapt upon the sleeping form, hugging it about its middle.

"Wretched!" she cried happily.

The bed's occupant was shocked out of a sound sleep and bounded up to grapple with its attacker, sending them both to the floor in a tangle of bedclothes and mosquito netting.

After a frantic scramble, two heads burst from beneath the linens, one shouting, "What are *you* doing here?" at the same time the other shouted, "Who the devil are you?"

Joe continued, "You're not Wretched!"

"As many ladies with ... intimate knowledge of me will attest," said Aaron Matthews with a grin.

They began untangling themselves from the bedclothes, Joe with the object of getting out of them—Aaron with the object of keeping at least a portion of them wrapped about his loins. The girl was fully clothed, but Aaron had been sleeping in the nude. Even in winter the nights were tropically warm on Key West.

"This is Richard's room!" declared Joe.

"Dear me, I understood it to be vacant. At least, that is what Captain Thibodeaux indicated when he let it to me last evening." Aaron finally succeeded in disengaging himself from her. He sat (appropriately swathed) on the bed while Joe backed across the room to press her posterior against the door.

"I had the impression from your parents," said Aaron, "that while your father and all the other wreckers were racing to the reef to save my unfortunate *St. Gertrude*, good old Wretched Richard was sneaking off to join the Glorious Army Of The Confederacy."

Joe was pressing door splinters into her backside in her haste to get out of the room. "I'm going turtling before it gets too light. I only came to get the poking stick ... here it is ... I'm sorry I disturbed you, Mister ..."

"Matthews. Joe, isn't it?"

"I gotta go. It'll be light." With that she slipped out the door and closed it behind her.

Aaron snatched up his clothes, from the chair where he had piled them, and jigged into them.

END OF SAMPLE CHAPTERS
OF
MUDSILLS & MOONCUSSERS
BY
IRIS CHACON

DUBY'S DOCTOR

*A spinsterish surgeon is blackmailed int[o]
caring for an amnesiac with the body of a[n]
Adonis and the mind of a child. She will s[ee]
that he learns to read and write, and he will s[ee]
that she learns what she has missed by living h[er]
solitary existence.*

*Neither of them knows the man w[as]
formerly an undercover agent, and they'll bo[th]
learn the meaning of danger when his old enem[ies]
catch up with him. In the ultimate confrontatio[n]
will the couple know how to fight back an[d]
survive?*

PROLOGUE

As he fell, he wondered why he had once again jumped from a perfectly good aircraft. He assumed it was perfectly good because he heard the helicopter's rotor blades beating the air as its engine noise moved off into the distance somewhere above him.

Half-formed thoughts lumbered through his muggy brain.

Pain.

Pain screamed through every nerve ending of his body. So much of it, he couldn't even pinpoint its source.

Cold.

Wind whipped at bare skin as he fell.

Where are my clothes?

Self-preservation bellowed at him from deep within a mind-shrouding fog, *"Look down, Dilbert!"*

He seemed to be stretched out on his back in the air; he fought the up-rushing wind stream to turn his head slightly. In his peripheral vision, Caribbean blue ocean stretched in all directions.

"Prepare to hit the water!" Self-preservation yelled.

He tried to pull himself into a tight ball, rather than smack the surface like a pancake, possibly breaking every bone in his body. If he could become a hydrodynamic object, and if he hit the water at a good angle, and if he could manage to swim or at least float an undetermined number of miles, he just might survive this. *Whatever this was.*

He tried to wrap his arms around his knees and pull them into his chest, but one knee wasn't following instructions. One leg bent toward his torso as he ordered, but the other leg was AWOL for all intents and purposes, being dragged along for the ride. Oh, well, he'd just do the best he could.

Impact was sudden, loud, and painful at a level he had never dreamed possible. He was mildly aware of being warmer now that he was underwater instead of plummeting through air. But the altitude from which he had fallen, combined with his weight concentrated into a small irregular ball, sent him many meters beneath the surface.

Briefly he hung suspended, virtually weightless, in a womb of warm, salty water. He sensed, close at hand, a great darkness that promised relief from the horrible pain if he would only relax and let endless blackness swallow him.

"Up! Up! Air! Air!" shouted Self-preservation.

Leave me alone. I just want to sleep.

"Kick!" Self-preservation insisted. *"Kick your feet! Move your arms! Go up! Up!"*

Reluctantly he forced his limbs to move, though it seemed not all of them obeyed. Still, he followed the bubbles rising from his mouth and nose, and he defied the pain and blackness, until his head broke the water's surface. Involuntary gasps siphoned air into his aching lungs again and again until he was breathing almost normally.

"Float," was the last word Self-preservation uttered.

Lying on his back, the man floated upon the gently rolling sea and let his mind fade into the welcoming darkness.

He neither knew nor cared whether he would somehow survive the hours and miles of sea that lay between himself and the nearest land.

CHAPTER 1 – AIRBORNE

At dawn over Elliot Key, seagulls glided across the pink-blue pastel streaks of sunrise mirrored in the glassy blue-silver ocean. Waves swished against the soft sand that fringed the island, and a sailboat sloughed at its anchor cable. Against the eastern sky, the boat's tri-corn sail formed a romantic silhouette against the sky, while its three-sided shadow doppelganger rippled on the surface of the water.

Halfway between the sailboat and the shore a honeymooning couple rowed their dinghy toward the beach. She giggled at something he said. He crooned something seductive. She laughed and swatted him playfully.

Miami city lights adorned the northwestern horizon like a diamond choker, two dozen miles away as the osprey flew.

Gulls cawed to one another, the sea gurgled against the shore, and the honeymooners' oars softly slapped the water. A breeze off the ocean rustled dry palm fronds. A four-foot-tall blue heron stood sentinel among flying buttresses of mangrove roots.

When they reached the shore, the couple dragged their little boat shushing across the sand onto the beach, beyond the water's grasp. They kissed beneath the rustling palms, and when they stepped apart, the man tickled the woman.

She twisted away, laughing and scolding, and ran from him, come-hither fashion. He pursued. They left two sets of footprints in the dimpled sand as they trotted like children along the beach in the pale dawn.

From time to time the mangrove trees' arching roots crept all the way to the water line, forcing the couple to detour into ankle-deep surf and come back to the sand. At one such spot, the woman was several yards ahead of the man because he had stopped to examine a nearly intact conch shell. She worked her way from sand to water, wading around a mangrove root, and glanced back at her pursuer.

He straightened from his shell collecting and winked at her.

She giggled and turned to look ahead of her again. As she rounded the mangrove, she screamed.

The man reacted to her scream and doubled his pace. He found her standing rigidly beside the mangrove, screaming again and again. He took in the situation and, with protective arms around her, he turned, putting himself between her and the source of her horror: a man's naked body sprawled face down, tangled in the arching tree roots.

A bedside telephone rang at the home of Frank and Mandy Stone. Frank reached across Mandy's impression of Moby Dick in curlers. He lifted the receiver and answered with a sleepy grunt.

"Monitoring per your orders, sir," said a young man. "I think the Coast Guard has your boy out on Elliot Key."

"Alive?"

"Uncertain, sir. They're airlifting to Jackson Trauma Center."

"Well done. Thanks for the call." Frank replaced the receiver and sank back onto his pillow. He said a short, silent prayer for a miracle, then he rose and began to dress.

Inside a Coast Guard helicopter two medics worked efficiently over an unconscious man. One medic bandaged a head wound while the other splinted and wrapped the man's left leg.

"Femoral artery remained intact. That's the only reason he didn't bleed out. But somebody's got their work cut out rebuilding this leg."

Suddenly the first medic stopped bandaging, felt for a pulse, and swiftly began chest compressions. "May not have to rebuild anything," the medic said. "I've lost him again."

While one rescuer performed cardio-pulmonary resuscitation, the other administered oxygen and verified the intravenous feed was working.

The first medic chanted in time with his rib-crunching thrusts, "*Come* on, man; *work* with me; *pump* for me; *you* can do it."

Minutes later the Coast Guard helicopter landed on the roof of Jackson Memorial Trauma Center. White-coated hospital personnel rushed to the aircraft with a gurney, everyone ducking the still-spinning rotors and resultant dust storm. The two Coast Guard medics helped transfer their patient to the gurney, and one of them followed the team into the building to provide a detailed briefing if necessary.

Such briefings were not often needed now that vital signs and treatment information could be transmitted to the hospital directly from the helicopter, but the personal touch was still appreciated. And occasionally there were questions. Given the circumstances, there were bound to be questions about this unidentified patient, but there would be few, if any, answers.

CHAPTER 2 – STONE

Frank Stone was not a handsome man on a good day, and this was not a good day. He strode into the trauma center emergency room looking rumpled and sleepy, in a gray polyester suit from Sears. The suit needed cleaning.

He took off his sweaty jacket and revealed his short-sleeved white dress shirt, which he wore with a clip-on bow tie. Shirt buttons strained to cover a beer belly. Frank wore white socks with brown loafers, both nearly covered by the droopy cuffs of slacks that rode beneath his belly, several inches lower than his natural waistline.

No one had ever guessed his age within five years, but people always thought him old enough to know what he was doing.

While not handsome, Frank was winsome in his way. He gave the appearance of a well-used, long-loved teddy bear whose stuffing was lumpy from years of hugging. Nothing about Frank Stone's appearance seemed threatening. When people met him for the first time, his looks were his initial lie, to be followed inevitably by many more.

Stone wove a path through the emergency room's rushing interns, nurses, orderlies, and aides, past a waiting room filled with patients and their families, to the registration desk. There, upon his inquiry, a nurse pointed him toward treatment rooms at the rear, where curtains were drawn around a crowded, noisy cubicle.

A female in surgical scrubs emerged from the curtained cubicle, carrying a chart. Stone nabbed her with a big paw on her elbow.

"Is he talking?" Stone asked.

"Are you family?"

Stone fished a wallet from the pocket of his slouchy pants and showed the woman his federal identification. "Uncle," he said. "Has he said anything? A name? Anything?"

She shook her head. "He's way under."

"You don't know the half of it," said Stone, pocketing his wallet. "How long before I can talk to him?"

She sighed with exhaustion. She had been on duty all night, and this new patient would keep her in the operating room most of the day.

"You'll have to ask the neurology boys that one," she said. "I'm just here to rebuild the leg – mostly the knee – if he makes it. What's his name, 'Uncle'?"

"I can't say."

She sighed again. "Second John Doe we've had since midnight." She nodded to the adjacent cubicle, where no one was working on the patient. "And our average isn't good, so far."

Stone perked up with new interest. "You had another John Doe last night?"

She nodded. Then, in response to a gesture from Stone, the doctor showed him into the dead John Doe's cubicle. A body on a gurney was draped completely. Stone walked to the head of the gurney, lifted the sheet, and looked at the man's ashen, lifeless face.

Then he dropped the sheet, moved to the foot of the gurney, and lifted the covering over the corpse's feet. A toe tag identified the man as "John Doe."

"Whattaya know about this guy?" asked Stone.

"Homeless. Hit and run on I-95 near Biscayne. Looks like he'd been living under the overpass."

Stone snatched the toe tag off the body and shoved it into the doctor's hands.

"For the record, and for the press, I hereby officially identify this *dead* man as Special Agent Yves Dubreau of the Federal Department of Homeland Security. He has obviously been the victim of a freak fishing accident while on annual leave." Stone pointed to the cubicle where multiple professionals were attempting to stabilize the man brought in by Coast Guard helicopter. "*That* one is John Doe. *Comprende?*"

Dr. Mitchell Oberon stared in horror at this scruffy man, whom she liked less with every passing second. Mitchell led the life of a prudish spinster with time for little outside her work; she kept her person and her surroundings clean and tidy. She drove the speed limit exactly, stopped for yellow lights, followed rules to the letter. This sloppy, round, absurdly demanding person wanted her to flout the law. It was almost incomprehensible to her. Speechless, she turned and led Stone out of the dead man's cubicle.

Mitchell took Stone to the admitting desk, where she retrieved the medical chart for the corpse. She shook the chart in Stone's face.

"The answer is no. First of all, that would be lying, and I don't lie. Second, if I did what you're asking me to do, I could be in serious trouble for falsifying medical records," she said.

"Not. *Asking.*" Stone spoke barely above a whisper. "Listen very carefully, Doctor: Some very bad people want this guy dead."

He pointed to the cubicle of the injured man. "So, he better be well and truly dead. 'Cause you ain't seen trouble until the bad guys learn he *ain't* dead, and they come in here looking to correct their little oversight."

He picked up a pencil from the admitting desk and tapped the chart belonging to the dead man. "Besides, you won't get in trouble for doing what the law requires you to do. And today I am The Law. Now, mark the chart."

Mitchell glared at the determined man. "Even if the law is willing to overlook it, my conscience will know what I've done is wrong."

He stared at her.

"Let me see that badge again."

He stared at her while he again took out his wallet and flipped it open to reveal his official identification.

Mitchell studied the badge carefully. She was ninety per cent certain it was the real thing. She recalled all the news stories she had read and heard about the nearly limitless power of the DHS. They said even the FBI and CIA had no standing to curb the activities of Homeland Security. She lifted her gaze from the man's badge to his visage.

He stared at her.

As she looked into his face, she felt cold fingers of fear tickling the edges of her mind. Her brow crinkled. "Are you telling me I really don't have a choice?"

He stared at her.

So she took the pencil from him grudgingly and began to erase the name "John Doe" from the dead man's chart. "You'll have to spell that agent's name for me," she said.

On the edge of Coconut Grove loomed an impressive Mediterranean-style mansion with castle-like towers and tile-roofed cupolas. Broken glass studded the top of the stone wall surrounding the estate. All its metal gates were electrified.

A muscular man patrolled inside the wall with a leashed attack dog. As he passed the swimming pool, he waved to the armed sentry who paced in a tower overlooking the pool and tennis court.

Kyle Averell enjoyed an elegant breakfast on a vast teak deck with a view of the courts, where his adult daughter, Carinne, and her coach, Trish, were playing a half-hearted tennis match. Averell looked up when his bodyguard, Rico, emerged from the house with the morning paper.

Rico folded the paper carefully and placed it before his boss, jabbing at a news item with one heavy finger.

Averell put his coffee cup down and picked up the article to read. A moment later he replaced the paper on the table and lifted his coffee cup toward the waiting carafe. As Rico refilled his *jefe*'s cup, Averell commented with mock sentimentality.

"Oh dear, oh dear. A Homeland Security agent killed – while on a fishing vacation, of all things. How ironic to survive vicious terrorists and criminals only to be done in by a trout. Life is cruel."

More sternly, he added: "Carinne will not see the papers today."

"I'll take care of it, Mr. Averell."

Down on the tennis court, Trish was shouting cheerily at her opponent, attempting to generate enthusiasm. Averell watched them as Rico took the newspaper away. Carinne seemed weary of the game and of life in general. He hoped his daughter would not become the sort of problem her unfortunate mother had been.

END OF SAMPLE CHAPTERS
OF
DUBY'S DOCTOR
BY
IRIS CHACON

Made in the USA
Charleston, SC
11 January 2017